"I'm not Malcolm."

Harper didn't take her eyes from the man as she said, "I know."

He might look like her boss, but there was an intensity in every part of him—from his gaze to the way he held himself—that easygoing Malcolm had never had.

Then she remembered a little-discussed feature of Tate Armor Ltd.—it was jointly owned by Malcolm and his brother.

"You're twins," she whispered and he nodded.

All the pieces finally fit into place. She'd been confused about why she'd never been drawn to her boss before the night of the masked ball, and why he hadn't stirred a reaction in her since.

But she'd made love with *Nick* that night. Things between them had happened so fast that even though she'd thought she'd sensed something different about him, she hadn't had time to stop and question it. He'd kissed her and she'd melted and all coherent thought had ended.

And it was also why Malcolm had been able to act like nothing had happened when she saw him the next morning at work. Nothing *had* happened with him. Nick, on the other hand... Well, he'd rocked her world.

* * *

Tempted by the Wrong Twin is part of the series Texas Cattleman's Club: Blackmail—No secret—or heart—is safe in Royal, Texas...

Dear Reader,

I've always been fascinated by the masks we wear. You know, the ones we put on to show people the image of us we want them to see. The ones we wear to hide the things we don't want to share.

Harper Lake works hard to appear—and to be—calm, self-sufficient and in control. She doesn't like anyone getting under her skin. But Nick Tate is wearing an even more impenetrable mask—one that pretends that he's okay after surviving the horrors of war.

It was interesting to see these two guarded people cope when they're thrown together. After meeting at a masked ball (of course!) three months earlier, they're now in a situation where they'll have to remove the masks they wear for other people if they want a chance at a future together. The question is, are they brave enough to be vulnerable with each other?

If you'd like some behind-the-scenes glimpses into this book, drop by my website, rachelbailey.com.

I hope you enjoy Nick and Harper's story!

Rachel

RACHEL BAILEY

TEMPTED BY THE WRONG TWIN

 HARLEQUIN® DESIRE

Special thanks and acknowledgment are given to Rachel Bailey for her contribution to the Texas Cattleman's Club: Blackmail miniseries.

Recycling programs for this product may not exist in your area.

ISBN-13: 978-0-373-83861-5

Tempted by the Wrong Twin

Copyright © 2017 by Harlequin Books S.A.

Printed in U.S.A.

Rachel Bailey developed a serious book addiction at a young age (via Peter Rabbit and Jemima Puddle-Duck) and has never recovered. Just how she likes it. She went on to earn degrees in psychology and social work but is now living her dream—writing romance for a living.

She lives with her hero and four dogs in a piece of paradise on Australia's Sunshine Coast, where she loves to sit with a dog or two, overlooking the trees and reading books from her ever-growing to-be-read pile.

Rachel would love to hear from you and can be contacted through her website, rachelbailey.com.

Books by Rachel Bailey

Harlequin Desire

Claiming His Bought Bride
The Blackmailed Bride's Secret Child
At the Billionaire's Beck and Call?
Million-Dollar Amnesia Scandal
Return of the Secret Heir
Countering His Claim

The Hawke Brothers

The Nanny Proposition
Bidding on Her Boss
His 24-Hour Wife

Texas Cattleman's Club: Blackmail

Tempted by the Wrong Twin

Visit her Author Profile page at Harlequin.com, or rachelbailey.com, for more titles.

This book is for Amanda Ashby,
who is most excellent at brainstorming,
can both cheer and cajole (often simultaneously!),
has good taste in TV shows, makes a
mean bliss ball and writes amazing books.

Bunches and bunches of thank-yous to
the awesome Charles Griemsman for, you know,
pretty much everything. Also, thank-you hugs for
Barbara DeLeo and Sharon Archer, who read early
drafts of this book and had fabulous suggestions.
And to my fellow TCC authors—it's been fun!

One

When his twin brother's name flashed on his cell phone screen, Nick Tate accepted the call—it was pretty much the only number he didn't let go through to voice mail these days.

Before he could even offer a greeting, Malcolm's voice thundered, "Goddammit, Nick. You slept with our lawyer, didn't you?"

The blood in his veins froze. There was only one woman he'd slept with since he'd returned from his last tour of duty, and they hadn't stopped to share life histories. They hadn't even stopped to exchange names. And now it seemed as though that had been a mistake.

"She's our lawyer?" he asked. Maybe he'd misheard.

"Harper Lake has been Tate Armor's company attorney for just over two years."

Nick winced. That was the problem with being a silent partner in their business—he missed out on all the details. And it turned out that their lawyer was one hell of an amazing detail. It had been three months since their night together and he still hadn't stopped thinking about her, but he'd had no way to track her down. Until now.

"And," Malcolm continued, "it seems you didn't tell her who you were. She thinks she slept with me."

Nick swore under his breath. Most people couldn't tell them apart at the best of times, but add a half-face mask—since it had been a masked ball—and his pretending to be Malcolm, and the task would have been virtually impossible. They hadn't switched identities since they were kids, but when Nick had heard that a disgruntled customer had threatened his twin and would be stalking him at the ball, he didn't hesitate to step in and make things right. It had been going on for several weeks, and enough was enough. He might not be good for much anymore, but this was something he could fix for his brother. Even if it had meant dragging his sorry ass out of seclusion.

So, yeah, since Harper knew Malcolm, she must have mixed Nick up with him that night. He just hadn't realized it at the time. Their connection had been instant and explosive, and there hadn't really been time to explain. Or even make it to the bed.

Despite the annoyance emanating from his brother

on the other end of the phone, Nick smiled at the memory. He'd never met anyone remotely like Harper Lake.

But now wasn't the time for reminiscing. He pulled himself together and addressed the problem at hand. A rare night of letting go had created consequences for his brother, the twin who'd always had enough finesse and charm for them both.

"I'll handle this, don't worry." Now that he knew her name and where she worked, he'd be able to talk to her. Maybe he could wait for her after work tomorrow. Or perhaps he could drop in at lunch and offer—

"This isn't some simple glitch that you can ride in on your white horse and sort out, Nick."

Something in Malcolm's voice had Nick's SEAL training kicking in, and his entire body went on alert. "What do you mean?"

"Harper's pregnant."

The power of the word hit him square in the chest. *Pregnant?* Only his training kept him on his feet as the world tilted around him.

Harper was pregnant with his baby.

And then a second wave hit him with even more force than the first. *Ellie.* His three-year-old daughter—the only reason his heart still beat after the horrors of war had pummeled it—could suffer the fallout of his behavior. His ex-wife's lawyers would use this to further their case that he was an irresponsible and unfit father. Especially if they knew the circumstances of how he'd swapped identities with his brother. His temples throbbed, and he rubbed them with his free hand.

Dammed if he was going to let them take Ellie from him. He'd fix this. Fix it for all of them.

He jerked his wrist over to check his watch. It was almost seven. "Are you at work? Is Harper still there?"

"She just left," Malcolm said. "She waited until everyone else had gone for the day and came into my office. She said she wanted me to know and offered to do a paternity test if I wanted."

He could see the scene playing out in his mind, and he hated it. Hated that he'd put his brother in that awkward position, but mostly hated what he'd done to Harper. What must she be feeling? Cursing him—or the Malcolm version of him—at the very least. She was probably overwhelmed.

He had to swallow hard to get his voice to work. "Did you tell her you weren't at the masked ball? That it was me?"

"I said I had to go, apologized and promised we'd talk about it in the morning. She seemed taken aback, but I figured it was your job to tell her."

"You figured right." This situation was complex enough without her getting the details from his brother.

"You know how dangerous this is, don't you?" Malcolm said, his voice a note lower than it had been. "You're an owner of the business, and sexual harassment cases are no laughing matter."

"Yeah, I get it." Nick had always been responsible, even when he was a kid, so he'd never thought he'd be the guy his brother would have to give this talk to, and it sat uncomfortably.

"Plus, with this Maverick guy going around town spilling everyone's secrets, don't count on this situation being private for long. He might already know."

Nick frowned. He might have been out of the loop, but even he had heard about the blackmailer causing headaches and heartaches for people all over Royal. Still, it was a little premature to be thinking about interference here.

"How could he possibly know when I only just found out?"

"How did he know that Wes Jackson had a kid with Isabelle Grayson? How did he know about Cecilia Morgan's background? He's obviously got some serious hacking and investigative skills."

"True," Nick said on a sigh. Local businessman and manufacturer Wesley Jackson was a friend of Malcolm's and Nick had met him a few times. Wes and Isabelle were decent people who hadn't deserved what Maverick had put them through.

"Also, all Maverick's targets seem to be in the TCC, and since you and I are both members, we can't discount the risk."

"Hell." Malcolm had a point. And the new proposals he'd been working on for the supply of body armor were all for security agencies. Given the nature of their business, handing Maverick ammunition to use on them in the form of a scandal like this would make them look like amateurs.

He blew out a breath. "Our clients need to know that any information they give us about their organizations is secure and not susceptible to a hacker."

"Yeah," Malcolm said, sounding weary. "Now is the time to have everything aboveboard. No secrets that could make us vulnerable."

"I'm on it." Nick grabbed his Kevlar riding jacket and slid his arms in, one at a time, switching the cell to his other hand as he went. "I'm going to need her home address."

"It's in Pine Valley. I'll text it to you."

"Thanks. And Malcolm?" he said, glancing up at the ceiling.

"Yeah?"

Nick drew in a long breath and held it for a moment before replying. "I will handle this. I'll make everything right." There was no other option. He'd make things right for Ellie, for Harper, for Harper's baby, for Tate Armor—for everyone.

"Good luck."

Nick disconnected the call, grabbed his wallet and keys and headed out the door. Hell would freeze over before he'd ever let down someone he was responsible for again.

But by the time he'd reached Harper's place— a "country cottage" that was far too impressive to deserve such a description—he was having doubts. How was he even going to convince her that he, not Malcolm, was the father of her baby?

Hi. You might be interested to learn that Malcolm has an identical twin brother.

Nope.

Hey, Harper. Remember that night you thought you

*were with Malcolm and conceived his baby? Well, it
was me. Surprise!*

Not even close.

*Harper, I have something to say and you might
want to sit down. My name is Nick, and I was im-
personating my twin brother when we met. I should
have told you before things got out of hand, and I
apologize.*

He'd need to find much better words in the next
thirty seconds or risk having the door slammed in
his face.

He knocked on her front door, still having no idea
how he could possibly explain everything. Then the
door swung inward and she was there and he had no
air left to form words anyway. Her almond-shaped
brown eyes widened at the sight of him, and he knew
he had to say something. Anything. But her haunting beauty overwhelmed him. He'd barely been able
to stop thinking about her since that night, and now
here she was in real life. Filling his vision. Smelling
like heaven.

"Malcolm?" she said, her voice breathy, and instead of explaining, he found himself mute, reaching
out to feel the silky-soft skin of her cheek. His palm
cupped the side of her jaw, his fingers feathering over
her cheekbone, and he was lost.

Her eyes widened in surprise and she took a small
step back, out of his touch, but her gaze didn't falter.
He waited a beat, waited in agony, waited until she
swayed back toward him, and then he reached for her
again. Her lips parted as she tilted her head into his

palm. The world around them faded, and he took an infinitesimal step closer, being drawn by the magnetic force that had been there since he'd first laid eyes on her three months ago.

He was supposed to say something, tell her something, but there were no words in his mind, only Harper and the way her eyes had darkened as she looked at him. Breathing ragged, he lowered his head and speared his fingers through her long, glossy hair. This was wrong, so wrong, yet the *rightness* of it overwhelmed him, crushing all other thoughts.

She lifted herself on tiptoes and met him halfway, her mouth finding his, her lips soft, welcoming, wanting, her arms wrapping around his shoulders and gripping tight. With a groan of surrender, he slid his tongue along hers and hauled her flush against him.

This.

This was what had driven him crazy the night they'd met. This was what had kept her in his waking dreams since. This was what was making him dizzy now.

Of course, a little voice at the back of his mind whispered, this was also what had led him into trouble in the first place.

He had to stop kissing her. To find the strength to pull away and explain everything. Oh, but her mouth and what it was doing to his was divine…

Reluctantly, he eased back a little, then brushed his lips over hers one last time before straightening. She dropped her hands—all contact was broken—and he blinked hard to make his mind work. She gazed up at him, her eyes unfocused and her lips rosy from their kiss, and previous thought deserted him. In that moment, all that mattered was that Harper Lake knew she'd kissed *him*. Knew she'd made love with him. Nick Tate.

So, with his voice as rough as gravel, all he heard himself say was, "I'm not Malcolm."

Harper gripped the edge of the door for balance but didn't take her eyes from him as she said, "I know."

If there was one thing for sure in the world, it was that the man in front of her was not the man she'd spoken to less than an hour ago. He might look like her boss, but there was an intensity in every part of him—from his gaze to the way he held himself—that easygoing Malcolm had never had.

And now that she was paying more attention, his hair was shorter, and there was a tiny scar in one eyebrow. But how was that possible? Then she remembered a little-discussed feature of Tate Armor Limited—it was jointly owned by Malcolm and his brother, Nick. A brother none of the staff had met and many of whom wouldn't know existed.

"Twins," she whispered, and he nodded.

All the pieces finally fit into place—her world made sense again. She'd been confused about why she'd never been drawn to her boss before the night of the masked ball, and why he hadn't stirred a reaction in her since. But she'd made love with *Nick* that night. Things between them had happened so fast that even though she'd thought she'd sensed something different about him, she hadn't had time to stop and question it. He'd kissed her and she'd melted and all coherent thought had stopped.

And it was also why Malcolm had been able to act like they hadn't shared a night of passion when she saw him the next morning at work. At the time she'd been surprised—and relieved—that Malcolm had been able to carry on working with her as if they had an unspoken agreement to never mention their night together again. The first day had been awkward, but he hadn't batted an eye when she'd walked into his office with contracts for him to sign.

As if nothing had happened.

Because nothing *had* happened with him.

Nick, on the other hand…well, he'd rocked her world.

She drew in a long breath and gripped the door a little tighter.

Nick was watching her warily, waiting to see what her reaction would be. Or perhaps he'd been as disoriented by their kiss as she had. Either way, they needed to talk, and standing on her porch was not the place to do it.

"You'd better come in," she said as she opened the door wider and stepped back into the hall to let him pass.

Once they were in her kitchen, she made him a coffee and herself a peppermint tea—something that seemed to be keeping the morning sickness steady.

Nick accepted the steaming mug, set it on the

counter beside him and blew out a long breath. "Look, about the ball—"

"No need," she said, cutting him off. It wasn't something she wanted to revisit in the cold light of day. "We're beyond that now."

He shook his head sharply. "I have to say it. I should have been up front. Told you who I was."

Looking at him now, dominating her kitchen with no effort at all, she wondered how she could have confused the brothers, but hindsight was twenty-twenty.

"If I'd known Malcolm's brother was his identical twin, I might have put two and two together on the night. I've worked with Malcolm. He's attractive, sure, but he never made my knees go weak."

"And I do?" Nick said, a cocky grin forming on his lips.

"I think we've proven that. Twice now. But that's not what you're here to talk about."

The grin widened, then faded again. "I just wanted you to know that I wasn't deliberately deceiving you."

She arched an eyebrow. "You were there on Malcolm's ticket. That's pretty deliberate."

"That's a fair point," he said, wincing. "There was something I needed to do for Malcolm."

"Deal with his stalker?"

Nick's head jerked up and he met her gaze, surprise clear in his eyes. "You saw that?"

The whole staff at Tate Armor knew about the guy—an ex-customer—who'd been so angry at Malcolm personally that he'd begun to make threats. Malcolm, nice as ever, had been trying to use diplomacy to defuse the situation. No one else had believed that had a chance of working. And the fact that the entire town was on edge thanks to the blackmailer Maverick only made things worse. There were whispers in the office that the guy might be working for Maverick, but Harper had always thought it was unrelated—Maverick's modus operandi was completely different. Which had left them with a run-of-the-mill jerk who wasn't responding to Malcolm's way of dealing with the situation.

Then, at the masked ball, Harper had been fascinated when the man she thought was Malcolm had calmly but firmly laid down the law for the man. He hadn't even had to say much. It had been in his slightly menacing stance. In his lethal tone of voice. The troublemaker hadn't been happy, but he'd clearly known he was up against a brick wall and had let it go.

"Yes, I saw you. You were…formidable." He hadn't had to do anything sinister, but it had been obvious to both Malcolm's stalker and to her that Nick was almost entirely composed of tightly coiled energy only just held under control. It had scared one of them off. Harper, however, had pulled him out onto the dance floor and made love with him soon after. "But you still could have told me."

"I wasn't sure if you knew Malcolm. You never called me by his name, so I thought you were meeting me just as me. Besides," he said, his cocky grin back in place, "neither of us seemed to be in the mood for chitchat."

She sipped her peppermint tea and hoped he'd attribute the heat in her cheeks to the steam curling up from the drink and not from blushing at the memory.

"And I would have told you afterward, but you left in a hurry." He let the statement hang in the air—not quite an accusation, but clearly waiting for an explanation.

For a moment, she was back in the suite Nick had rented in the hotel where the ball was being held, straightening her clothes, mumbling an inadequate "I have to go" and trying not to break into a sprint, hoping Malcolm—Nick—didn't get his trousers on and catch up to her before she made it out to her car.

She didn't even meet his eyes as she said, "I suddenly realized I'd slept with my boss. There may have been some freaking out happening."

He considered that for a moment and waited until she looked at him before replying. "I get that. Although, at the time, not knowing the background, you could say I was somewhat surprised."

"It might have been different if I'd known you weren't my—" She didn't complete the sentence as the logic tripped her up. "Actually, you're still my boss. Just the silent partner at the company."

"True, but let's leave that aside for the moment." He took a mouthful of coffee, then put his mug on the counter and dug his hands in his pockets before meeting her gaze. "No excuses. I should have told you, and I apologize."

"Accepted," she said and blew out a breath, glad to leave the topic behind.

Nick picked up his coffee mug again and downed another mouthful. The silence was heavy with all that still sat unresolved between them, but she wasn't sure how to start now.

Finally, he said, "We'd better talk about what we're going to do."

She pushed off the counter she'd been leaning on and headed for the living room. "Come in and sit down." This conversation could go well or could be a disaster, and the only thing she had to help smooth the process was comfortable seating, which wasn't particularly reassuring.

"So, we're having a baby," he said without preamble once they were settled on the sofa.

She nodded, glad he'd brought the subject up. He'd obviously known she was pregnant—the timing of his appearance was too coincidental to mean anything else—but she was relieved not to have to announce the news for the second time in one night. "We are."

"I assume since you sought me—well, Malcolm— out, when you didn't have to, that you're planning on keeping it?"

"Yes." She'd turned in her seat so her back was against the armrest. She wanted to be able to see his reactions more easily and also create a little distance. Clearly she needed all the help with that she could get. "Are you on board with that?"

"Absolutely," he said without hesitation. "Don't doubt for a second that I want our baby."

Unease prickled across her skin. His gaze was deadly serious, and she didn't know him well enough to read him. Did he just mean that he didn't want her to end the pregnancy, or was there a more ominous message? Was Nick Tate the sort of man who might try to claim sole custody? This man was a stranger, and to a certain extent she was at sea in knowing how to handle him.

Her lawyer's sense of justice kicked in, pointing out that, by the same token, he had to be equally at sea with her. He was likely trying to read between the lines to discover all that she wasn't saying, so for now she should give him the benefit of the doubt.

She drew in a breath and said, "Two babies, actually."

His eyes widened. "Twins?"

"Yes."

He sat back with a thud. "Okay, we're having *two* babies." A smile tugged at the corners of his mouth and he seemed lost in thought for a moment before returning his focus to her. "How are you? Any morning sickness?"

Instinctively, she laid a hand over her stomach. "Only a little. I'm a bit queasy in the face of milk and greasy things, but not too bad."

"Does the doctor say everything is okay?" His gaze flicked from where her hand rested on her belly and back again.

"She said everything is perfectly normal." She tapped her fingers against her thigh, unsure of what else to say, then remembered that she had something she could show him. "I have a picture from the sonogram. Would you like to see it?"

He grinned. "You bet."

She pulled the printout from inside the pages of a large hardcover book on the coffee table and handed it to him. Since her appointment, she'd spent so much time staring at this picture in wonder. It was almost surreal—they were *her babies*, growing inside her right this minute. Despite knowing so little about them, her love for these tiny beings was so strong, it enveloped her, vibrating with power, practically a living thing itself.

Speaking past the emotion that filled her throat, she pointed out the same things the doctor had highlighted to her, then waited, fingers laced, while Nick had a moment to absorb the first image of their children.

When he handed it back, his eyes had misted over. "Thank you. That's...incredible."

She blinked back tears before they could fully form. "It is, isn't it?"

"If it's okay with you," he said, eyebrows drawn together, "I'd like to be at your future appointments."

The sense of unease returned. They were his babies, too—he had a right to know how they were doing. And of course she'd dreamed of having someone there to share the excitement and the fears, someone who understood what she was feeling, someone who would be a priceless support.

Still...she was the one who was pregnant, and having him attend her appointments, where she would be prodded and scanned and intimate details of her body would be discussed? Even contemplating that happening with a stranger in the room—albeit a stranger she'd slept with once... A shudder ran down her spine. It was too much, too soon.

"Nick, I want you to know that I won't keep the babies from you."

He nodded, as if she'd confirmed something for him. "Good, we're on the same page, because I plan to be involved."

It was just what she'd been hoping to hear from the father of her unborn children, and yet, it made it so much harder to deliver the news she had to tell him. She bit down on her lip, trying to find the perfect words.

"At some point during my pregnancy, I'll be moving home to Connecticut. I'm going to need my mother's support with the twins, but you'll be more than welcome to visit any time you want." Her mother had been the first person Harper had called when the stick had turned pink. And thank God she had—her mother had put everything into perspective for her, taking her from being overwhelmed to getting her head around her impending motherhood and believing she could do it. A big part of that had been her mother's offer to help her raise the twins. It was just what she'd needed to hear while she was panicking.

"Leaving?" he said, his tone a little sharper than it had been moments before. "You can't leave."

She laid a hand on his strong forearm, hating that she was doing this to him, but having no option. "I'm really sorry, Nick, but I honestly don't think I can do this without my mom's help."

He reached over and closed his hand over hers, holding it to his arm, infusing her hand with the warmth of his skin, sending her pulse into an erratic rhythm. "I already have a daughter. Ellie. I can't put into words how much I love her—she's the most perfect thing in my life."

Harper felt her mouth open, but she quickly caught the expression of surprise before it fully manifested. She wasn't sure why she was surprised he had a daughter—she knew so little about him that there could be much larger secrets and she'd have no idea.

"Ellie's a pretty name. She's lucky to have you."

"Well, that opinion's in the minority. Her mother—my ex-wife—is trying to keep her from me. That is not happening again. I want to be a hands-on dad with our babies."

Harper withdrew her hand from his grip and wrapped it around the nape of her neck. It was one thing for him to say he wanted to be hands-on, but they weren't a couple, and at the end of the day it would likely still be her on her own with newborns. She couldn't make this situation right for everyone. It was impossible.

Nick stood up in front of her, feet shoulder-width apart, hands on his hips. "Look, we've just met each other again, I've found out I'm going to be a father to twins and you've realized it was me and not Malcolm that night. This has been a big night for both of us."

"That's putting it mildly."

"How about we take some time to let this all sink in before we discuss the future? I'll come by tomorrow night and take you to dinner. We can talk more then."

Harper hesitated. If she had to make a guess, she'd say Nick wanted to take her out to soften her up so he could change her mind about moving away. Agreeing to dinner felt like going out under false pretenses when she knew she couldn't stay in Royal. But it was getting late, and he was right that it had been a big night. She'd been crashing into bed earlier now that she was growing two babies, and right now she was exhausted. All she wanted was to reheat some dinner and climb into her bed. So maybe putting the conversation on hold wasn't a bad idea.

She stood as well. "Sure, that sounds good."

"Great." He headed for the front door and paused with his palm resting on the handle. The memory of the way he'd greeted her when he'd arrived flooded her mind, and she wondered if he was thinking the same thing. If he'd kiss her again as he left.

But he simply said, "Is seven o'clock okay?"

Seven? Then her brain clicked back into gear. To pick her up. "Seven is good."

He gave her a guarded smile and opened the door. "See you then."

As she reached the door to close it behind him, he disappeared down the path and was gone. Barely an hour had passed since Nick Tate had exploded back into her life, and now everything was different.

And she was still unsure whether that was a good or a bad thing.

Two

The next night, Nick left for Harper's place with a bit of time to spare. He wanted to get her something, a token to show he was acting in good faith while they tried to work things through. Besides, she was in a tough place—pregnant with twins and thinking she had to leave Texas to get the support she needed. At least he could show her she was wrong about the last part.

He wanted a small gift, just to show he was here, ready to play his part. He'd heard some men bought their wives or partners jewelry when they became pregnant, but from the way Harper had reacted during their talk last night, he guessed a gift that expensive would overwhelm her. He just needed something to make her smile. Maybe he could start with flowers?

He ducked into the local grocery store and was confronted with rows and rows of buckets overflowing with blooms. And he hit the snag in his plan. In his experience, most women had a favorite flower, but he knew so little about Harper that he had no chance guessing. Sure, he knew more than he had twenty-four hours ago, but there were certain things that a man should know about the woman who was carrying his babies. Starting with her favorite flower...

"Dadddcc!" The sweet, familiar voice rang out and his heart melted into a puddle. He turned in time to catch his three-year-old in the air as she launched herself at him.

"Hey, beautiful girl," he said, squeezing her tight against his chest.

She leaned in to whisper in his ear. "Can you have dinner wiv us tonight?"

When she leaned back to see his face, her eyes were huge with entreaty, and it killed him to have to say no. Her mother, Melissa, and Melissa's fiancé wouldn't welcome him into their house, so even if he hadn't had plans with Harper, he would have to decline.

He glanced around, and sure enough, Melissa and Guy stood about ten feet away, both holding various grocery items, and neither smiling.

"Aw, baby, that's probably not a good idea. But I'll see you this weekend. How about we go to the park this time?"

Immediately distracted, Ellie nodded. "The big one wiv the swings?"

He grinned. "That's the one."

"I love you, Daddy," she whispered, gripping his neck tight.

"I love you, too, Ellie."

"Flowers. Are you going on a date, Nick?" Melissa was closer now. "You know I don't want girlfriends around Ellie. It's too disruptive for her. And my lawyer agrees."

Nick stifled the retort that sat on his tongue. He was perfectly capable of working out what was and wasn't good for his daughter. But getting into an argument in front of Ellie was definitely something that wouldn't be good for her.

"Nice to see you, Melissa." He tipped his chin at the other man. "Guy."

"I mean it, Nick," Melissa said, undeterred.

"You know what?" her smarmy fiancé said. "How about you go ahead and do it, and we'll have a much stronger custody case. Ellie tells us everything anyway."

Despite the pressure building in his head, Nick refused to rise to the bait. He gave Ellie another squeeze and put her down. "I'd love to stay and chat some more, but I have to go." He grabbed the closest bunch of flowers, said, "See you soon, baby," to his daughter, gave the adults a tight smile and headed for the checkout.

A few minutes later, he slid into the driver's seat of his car and paused before starting the engine. His lawyer had given him similar advice about women— if he was trying to prove that he was a stable influence in Ellie's life, then a parade of girlfriends would work against him. That had been such a nonissue at the time, he'd barely paid attention. But now...

...now a woman he barely knew was carrying his twins.

He didn't have to run it by his lawyer to know that this would make him look irresponsible. And, as Malcolm had said, there were no secrets in Royal with Maverick on the loose, so Melissa could find out any day. Added to the PTSD he'd struggled with since his last deployment, it might be enough for the judge to award full custody of Ellie to her mother instead of the shared custody he was asking for. He couldn't go on with only a day every two weeks with his daughter. His lungs squeezed tight.

He had to do something.

Something to make him look more stable.

He ran through scenario after scenario, but, really, there was only one solution.

If he and Harper were married, not only would he avoid any appearance of irresponsibility, but, in the judge's eyes, he'd have a stable family unit to offer Ellie. Turning a negative into a positive.

The more he thought about it, marriage would not only help him with the custody case, it would also keep Harper here in Royal so he could be involved in the babies' lives. It was a win-win.

But could he do it? Marry a woman who was practically a stranger? Could he convince her to do it?

Movement at the front of the store caught his attention. Ellie danced around Melissa's legs as they made their way out the door and toward their car.

His heart thumped hard. He'd do anything for that little girl. And he already felt the same about being a part of the twins' lives, too. For all three children, he'd do anything. Even marry someone he didn't love.

Decision made, he started the engine. Now he just had to convince Harper.

Glad he'd allowed extra time, he drove by the Texas Cattleman's Club, where he'd made the reservation for dinner tonight. A few extra touches would help when he proposed. At this stage all he had going for him was that he and Harper had enough chemistry to light the city, so he wanted to do anything extra he could to sway the odds in his favor. It wasn't much, but he'd been on missions with less auspicious beginnings. He'd make it work.

On the way in, he heard his name and turned to see the tall, solid form of Gabe Walsh stepping out of his car. Gabe was a former special agent with the FBI who now ran the Walsh Group, his family's private security firm. Before Gabe had taken over, the Walsh Group had bought their body armor from Tate Armor, and Nick was loath to lose their business. One of the proposals he was working on now was the first one for TWG with Gabe at the helm.

"Walsh," Nick said, waiting until the other man reached him, and then shaking his hand.

"Not often we see you out and about, Tate. Is this a special occasion?"

For a long moment, Nick considered telling him about Harper and the babies, trying to make it sound like casual chat, but really letting him know early in case Maverick released the information. At least that way it wouldn't look like a security breach; instead, it would just be old news.

But, in reality, there was no way to announce such large personal news to a work acquaintance in a parking lot and make it sound natural. And Gabe had been in law enforcement—dropping something like that with no context would make him suspicious.

So, instead, he worked the other angle. "Just checking on a reservation. Hey, have you been looking into Maverick?"

Gabe's head cocked to the side. "You know something?"

"Actually, I was hoping you would."

Gabe winced. "Nothing. But I sure would love to know who it is."

"You and everyone in town." They reached the front doors, and both men stopped. Nick thrust his hand out, and Gabe shook it. "Good to see you. I'll have that proposal to you in the next few days."

"Looking forward to it." Gabe went through the doors, and Nick let out a breath.

If there was about to be a breakthrough on the case, Gabe Walsh would know about it—he had connections everywhere. Which meant the situation with Harper was ripe for Maverick to milk or try to blackmail him over. The only way forward was to neutralize the potential threat before Maverick acted on it.

And that brought Nick back to the one way to resolve the situation on all fronts.

He had to marry Harper Lake.

* * *

Harper glanced across at Nick as he sat on the other side of their relatively secluded table at the restaurant in the Texas Cattleman's Club. The table had the same crisp white tablecloth, sparking crystal glassware and thick, luxurious napkins as the others, but theirs definitely had something extra. To start with, there was the cascading arrangement of tiny white roses, and gold cutlery instead of silver on the other tables. And Nick had arrived to pick her up with a bouquet of pink lilies, which she'd put in a vase before they'd left. It all gave her a sinking feeling that Nick was pulling out all the stops. And she was going to tell him she was leaving anyway...

She'd been thinking about tonight almost constantly since he'd walked out her door twenty-four hours ago, and knew Nick would try to use their dinner to convince her to stay, so she'd decided to share one of her deepest fears with him, to be completely up front about why she had to go. Maybe then he'd understand—even if he didn't like it—and wouldn't make it more difficult than it already was.

At the very least, she owed him an explanation of why she wouldn't risk staying and failing. Afterward, they could work out visitation arrangements and do their best to ensure the babies had a relationship with their father.

But she had a feeling Nick wasn't going to make it easy to leave him.

She glanced at him now, the strong column of his throat emerging from the collar of his charcoal dress shirt, his mouth that she knew from experience could take her to heaven, dark eyes that were smoldering as they watched her... She tore her gaze away and looked down at her place setting. Leaving this man would never be easy.

In the car, as if by unspoken consent, they'd tabled the discussion about their situation and instead talked about the town and people they both knew. But now they were at the restaurant, and Harper didn't want to put it off any longer. She needed to let him know where she stood before he started his pitch.

"Nick," she began then paused to find some air for her lungs. "This is not how I pictured having my first baby."

"It's not how I pictured having my second and third, but we can make it work." He seemed so sure, so confident he could make things right, and that broke her heart.

A waiter brought the two glasses of sparkling water they'd ordered, and Harper took a sip, both to help her dry mouth and to wait until they were alone again to resume the conversation.

"I need to explain something." She tucked her hair behind her ear and met his gaze. "I grew up in a broken home. My mother did a great job, but some experiences will leave a mark. I made a vow that I'd never subject a child to the same pain, confusion and self-blame that I felt growing up."

He cocked his head to the side, surveying her. "You don't come across as someone who's riddled with doubts."

"How do I come across?" she asked, despite herself. She didn't want to be sidetracked, but she was suddenly very interested in his opinion of her.

"When Malcolm talked about our attorney, he always said you were a go-getter. Someone who doesn't back down for anyone or anything. Of course, I didn't connect you to the person he was talking about until last night, but I'd have to say my initial assessment of you is the same."

That was the image she'd tried to project. More than that, it was the person she'd worked hard to become. But life was always more complicated than that.

She shrugged one shoulder. "Appearances can be deceiving. The tough persona is an invisible armor I developed against being abandoned and rejected." She hesitated, unsure how far to expose herself. But it was fair that he knew, that he understood. Despite her body wanting to fold itself up into a ball, she straightened her spine and went on. "It started back when my father left. The night he went, he was angry, maybe it was defensive, I don't know, but he took it out on me as well as my mother. My last memories of him are him yelling at me in our living room then walking out the door."

And despite the yelling, she'd followed him and thrown herself on the lawn outside, sobbing as his car drove away. She closed her eyes for long moments, trying to contain the emotions the memory always stirred up. The only sound was the clink of dishes from other tables and a low hum of distant conver-

RACHEL BAILEY   35

sation. She was almost scared to open her eyes in case she'd said too much. Given too much information too soon.

But she did open them and found Nick's understanding gaze resting on her.

He drew in a deep breath. "God, Harper."

She shook her head. "Believe me, I'm not telling you this for sympathy. In fact I haven't told a soul that story before."

"Then why are you telling me?" he asked.

"The thing is, that night triggered something for me. I don't handle abandonment well, and I've never been able to move past it." In fact, she'd been repeating the pattern through poor choices in men, dating guys who turned out to be commitment-shy to say the least. And so the cycle had continued. Being aware of what she was doing hadn't helped her stop it. "Knowing how debilitating fears like that can be and how instability when you're young can have lifelong effects, I've always wanted my children to only know the love and security of an intact family unit. That's not an option now, but I still need to do the best I can to make the household they grow up in secure."

"You don't have to leave to get that. We can do that right here."

"I'll never keep them from you, Nick. I know how tough it can be to be separated from family members. But these babies are going to need a stable unit around them. You and I can try to work something out, but let's be realistic. We've just met."

"Sure, we just met," he said, gaze not faltering.

"But we're not your garden variety of strangers. We're expecting babies together, Harper. Unusual circumstances call for unusual measures."

His reasoning was compelling, but still...

She lifted the spoon in her place setting and turned it in her fingers as she composed her thoughts, then lined it up neatly with the other cutlery again. "I wasn't ready for one baby, let alone two, and I know I'll have trouble coping with two babies with absolutely no experience. My mother will be there for us. Full-time. I'm really sorry, but the right thing for these babies is for me to move back to Connecticut."

The waiter came by and, after telling them the specials, took their order. Once he left, Nick picked up the conversational thread again.

"I appreciate you telling me that. It couldn't have been easy." He squared his shoulders. "And I'll be as honest with you in return. You need to know that I have post-traumatic stress disorder from my time in the Middle East, and I've pretty much been living as a hermit since I got back. But I'm changing things." Frown lines appeared across his forehead. "I need to change things. My ex-wife is getting remarried, and she wants me to sign over my parental rights to our three-year-old daughter."

"That's crazy," Harper said, her lawyer's sense of justice kicking in. "Why would she want to keep a father and child from seeing each other?"

He speared his fingers through his hair. "She's claiming my PTSD is making me an unfit father."

"Is it?" she asked and tried not to hold her breath as she waited for the answer.

"No." His voice was clear and sure. "I might be screwing up a heap of things in my life, but Ellie isn't one of them. I'd do anything for her. Plus, she needs her father. She needs me. But—" he winced "—having two babies on the way with someone I'm not in a relationship with will probably damage my case."

"Oh, Nick." She hadn't thought the situation could be any more complex. She'd been wrong.

"There's something else we need to consider. With Maverick active and causing people real grief, this is a secret that may be released at an inopportune time."

Maverick. She hadn't even considered herself a possible target before—there had been nothing juicy enough in her life to interest him—but now she was just the sort of target he seemed to like. "If he announces that I'm pregnant by the boss, it would reflect badly on Tate Armor. It has the whiff of a workplace tinged by sexual harassment."

"Worse than that. The breach of privacy itself would make the company look like we don't know what we're doing in the security field."

"Of course," she said, running through the ramifications. "So we need to tell people ourselves soon so we're controlling the information."

"Ideally, yes. And if we ensure that everything looks unquestionably aboveboard, all the better."

"How can we do that?"

"The way I see it, we have a few problems that have arisen from this pregnancy. You're feeling overwhelmed and in need of backup. You also want an intact family unit for the babies. And I have to consider that I'll look irresponsible when my custody case is heard. And finally, Tate Armor's reputation is at risk."

She winced. "That does sound like a lot when you list everything out."

"I've thought about this, and I see one solution that addresses all of these problems."

"That must be a pretty powerful solution."

"It is." He rolled his shoulders back. "We should get married."

She coughed out a laugh. "Are you serious?"

"Very much. Think about it—you'd have my commitment that I'll be in this with you one hundred percent. You'll have all the backup you need without having to leave town. A hands-on father is the only way I know how to do it, anyway. The babies get two parents. Our relationship would look like a positive in my court case. And Tate Armor would be safe from Maverick. Everybody wins."

Everybody wins?

"Nick, we don't even know each other." It seemed like a point too obvious to say, but apparently it did need to be said aloud. Maybe this was the one detail he hadn't factored into his solution?

He tilted his head, conceding the point. "And if this was a first date, that would be a reasonable objection. But you're having my babies." His entire body stilled, but his eyes blazed with focus. "Marry me."

She leaned back in her the chair, heart racing double time. Marriage? It was too much. He was watching her closely, expression expectant, obviously thinking there was a chance she'd say yes. "Still, it's a really big step, Nick." Her gut was churning just thinking about it. "*Really* big."

"Also," he said, and the corners of his mouth tugged into a half smile as if he knew he was starting to bring her around, "my mother raised twins. She's here in town, and she'll be over the moon about our babies. She'll help out as much as we want. And if you want your mother around, too? No problem— we'll fly her down."

Harper sucked her bottom lip into her mouth and bit down on it. Marrying without love hadn't been in her life plan, but neither was being pregnant with twins. Nick was clearly committed to being a father to their children... Oh, God, was she seriously considering it? Her pulse felt erratic under her skin. It was completely ridiculous. Wasn't it?

"I've had a pregnant wife before, and even though I wasn't home through all of her pregnancy, I know there are things I can do to help."

"What sort of things?" she asked, curious. She'd spent the first three months of this pregnancy alone, and her thoughts had often strayed to how the experience would be different if she were part of a couple.

He shrugged. "Going to the store for olives at two in the morning. Massaging feet. Help with the heavier chores and picking things up from the ground. Just the regular things a pregnant woman might want."

Massaging feet? Ducking out for whatever she wanted to eat? She smiled. "That does sound useful." But her smile faded as she thought about the reality of their situation. "Nick—"

"I know we can do it," he said. "I love babies and kids. When Ellie was a baby, I was between tours, and her mother and I shared all her care. We can do this."

Try as she might, she couldn't see it working, but her legal training wouldn't let her ignore the fact that it was the only solution on the table that addressed each issue they faced, so she owed it to herself and the babies to at least give the idea due consideration.

She smoothed her skirt over her lap. "Did you see us living together?"

"Absolutely," he said, seemingly unfazed by her zeroing on the specifics.

"Are you thinking we'd live at your place or mine?"

"Mine. There's more room."

She almost smiled at the irony that they worked for the same company, yet she would commute to the company's office each morning and he would stay in the house she also lived in.

Then she realized she hadn't even seen his place. It could be a cabin in the woods with no running water. "Hang on. What's your place like?"

"Big. Just outside town." He rubbed a hand over his jaw as he thought. "Modern. Everything inside was done by a decorator, and she used words like *minimalist* and *sleek*. You can make any changes you want. I'm not fussy about that sort of thing."

"Can I ask you something?" Did she imagine the wariness flickering briefly in his eyes before he answered?

He sat back and picked up his glass of water. "Sure."

She laced her fingers together and, for a moment, wished her lawyer's heart could just *go with the flow* instead of insisting she gather all the facts to file neatly in their slots.

"If we went ahead with this plan, do you see us as a couple?"

He chuckled. "We would be married. That's pretty much the definition of a couple."

But it was an important issue—just *how* married did he want to be? "That's the legal arrangement. And we've discussed physical arrangements for me to move in. But what about us as two people?"

He raised an eyebrow. "You mean lovemaking?"

"I do," she said. "It's a reasonable consideration since we're not strangers on that front."

"No, we're not." A small muscle twitched in his jaw. "I'm open to the idea of a consummated marriage."

Her skin heated. She swallowed. Hearing him say the words brought memories racing to the fore. Memories of their bodies sliding against each other, of sensitized skin, of the sounds he made as he found his release.

The waiter reappeared with their meals, and Harper was thankful for the timing so she could regain her poise. There was no doubt he made her melt inside. And they already knew they had explosive chemistry. But things were different now—so much more entwined and complex. Would that dampen some of the chemistry between them? Or would his touch always affect her?

She needed to move on, to stop thinking of his touch...

She cleared her throat. "What about length of time? Are you suggesting a lifetime commitment?"

"No, that would be unreasonable. Ideally it would last until our children were grown, but if we both made a commitment of, say, five years, we'd address all of our issues."

"Except the one about the intact family unit."

Nick reached out and covered her hand, his gaze softening. "It would never be the way it was with your father, Harper. Since we'd be going in with a businesslike arrangement, we'd be able to dissolve the union with little mess and drama. We'd prioritize the children and both have major roles in their lives. There would be no words in anger. Neither parent would just disappear."

He gave her hand a reassuring squeeze then released it and picked up his utensils to twirl a forkful of pasta.

Her skin immediately felt the absence of his touch, which seemed to highlight the inherent problem of having to deal with *his* absence at the end of their marriage. What if they came to the end of five years and she'd fallen in love with him? Would she be setting herself up for another abandonment?

The weight of everything they were discussing came crashing down on her shoulders, and she could barely keep herself upright. She couldn't do it. There had to be another way. There had to be.

She put her fork down, her dinner barely touched.

"I'm sorry, Nick, but I don't think marriage is the right way forward for us."

He stilled, eyes focused on her. "Do you have another solution?"

"Not yet," she said. She'd figure something out, though. She always did. "Give me a few days."

He shook his head. "With Maverick on the loose, we might not have the luxury of a few days."

She blew out a long breath, considering the factors. "Okay, give me twenty four hours."

"Sure. I can do that," he said and signaled the waiter.

The short moment of relief that his agreement granted her soon faded as she realized that she had one day to achieve the near impossible.

Pushing that thought aside, she picked up her handbag and squared her shoulders, ready to meet the challenge head on.

Three

By the next afternoon, after looking at the situation from every angle, Harper had to concede that Nick's plan was the only option that addressed all of their issues. If she moved to Connecticut, her mother would give her the support she wanted, and they'd form a little family unit—the twins, their mom and their grandma. But it would make Nick look bad in his case for shared custody of Ellie. She couldn't make a decision that solely benefited her babies and threw their half sister and father under the bus. It would also risk the reputation of Tate Armor, and not just for Nick's sake—she'd worked there for years and had a lot of loyalty to the company, to Malcolm and to the staff.

She'd brainstormed, even tried to match various

smaller plans together to achieve the outcomes, but it seemed only Nick's plan would deliver on all fronts.

Her heart had been heavy since the realization had dawned. Marrying a man she didn't love, a virtual stranger, simply wasn't the path she'd dreamed her life would take, even if he did make her pulse race every time she saw him. Or thought of him.

As she listened to the ringtone, waiting for Nick to answer, her brain was still frantically trying to come up with an alternative.

"Harper." His smooth, deep voice sent a wave of heat over her skin. "Have you made a decision?"

As no alternative had presented itself in the last thirty seconds, she closed her eyes and faced her fate. "I think you're right. Getting married is the best option we have."

He blew out a breath. "Thank you. And I'll do my best to ensure you don't regret this."

She appreciated the sentiment, but she had a feeling she'd just stepped into something that was bigger than both of them.

"I have a few contacts at city hall," she said, "so I'll see what I can do about fast-tracking our license just in case Maverick is on the scent."

"Good idea. Hang on." In the background she heard a door opening and closing before Nick spoke again. "Have you given any thought to when you'd like to move in?"

She needed some time to steel herself, but since part of the reason they were doing this was for appearances, she couldn't move in with him any later than their wedding day. "I'll need to take a day of vacation leave for the wedding, so we could do it then."

"Sure," he said. "That suits me."

They'd touched on the length of their marriage last night, and although it was a discussion she'd rather have face-to-face, she was unlikely to see him before the wedding—especially if she managed to speed up their license—and she'd rather they agreed before vows were exchanged.

"I was thinking, too," she said, "about how long we should commit to being married."

"And what did you come up with?"

"The five years you suggested is reasonable. I can't imagine I'll have any energy to date with two tiny humans at home, anyway." And it was hard to imagine any man affecting her the way Nick did with only a look. In fact, he might have ruined her for other men for life.

"Good to know I won't be cramping your style," he said, heavy on the sarcasm, along with a note of something else she couldn't quite put her finger on.

"That gives the babies a solid five years with us together, so they'll have a strong relationship with both of us."

"And," he added, his voice confident, "as long as we handle the divorce well, it shouldn't impact them too much."

She looked up at the ceiling. Nick was probably being overly optimistic, but she'd definitely do her best to make the transition seamless.

She paced from her kitchen through to her dining

room. There was one other issue they hadn't agreed
on—their love life. Nick had said at dinner that he
was open to the idea of a consummated marriage, and
then their meals had arrived, so she'd been saved from
having to give her view. She'd thought about it since,
but she still didn't know what she wanted. Correc-
tion. She knew she *wanted* him, but she wasn't sure
an active love life in a relationship they were trying
to keep practical was wise. She waited a beat, wondering if he'd raise the topic, but either he thought it
was decided, or he was waiting for her.

And instead of facing how they'd handle one of the
most important aspects of marriage head-on —and despite Nick's view of her as someone who didn't back
down from anyone or anything— she let it go. They'd
already agreed to marry, so it wouldn't change things
now. After the wedding? They could play it by ear.

So she simply said, "I'll let you know when I have
any information about the license."

"Till then," he said and disconnected the call.

Harper kept the cell in her hand an extra minute,
wondering why she'd flaked from discussing their
potential love life.

And, more importantly, what she would decide to
do once she was finally confronted with the option
of having Nick Tate in her bed.

Friday morning Nick arrived at his own wedding
at city hall, hoping like all hell that his bride would
turn up. She'd agreed to the plan, but reluctantly, so

he wouldn't have been completely surprised if she'd changed her mind.

Harper had managed to fast-track their civil ceremony and had phoned earlier in the week to share details, but it had been a short call. Just the details.

His gut had been in knots all morning thinking about whether she'd changed her mind. He'd shot off a text saying, Everything okay for today? and she'd replied Yes, which was somewhat reassuring, but he wouldn't relax until the vows were said and his ring was on her finger.

Squaring his shoulders, he walked into the small, carpeted waiting room and found her there, looking elegant, and his entire body practically sighed in relief. She wore a knee-length dove-gray skirt with a white silk blouse, her hair fell in dark, glossy waves down her back and her lips were painted a soft pink. He'd never seen anyone more beautiful.

"Late to your own wedding?" said a familiar voice beside him. Nick scowled at the interruption and turned to his brother, who was making a mock-concerned face. "Gee, I don't know, Harper. I think you could probably do better. Find someone who prioritizes you and your wedding enough to arrive on time."

"I'm not late. In fact, we're all early." Nick saw his mother beside Malcolm and stepped past his twin to embrace her. "Thanks for coming on short notice."

When he'd called with the news, she'd been staying with her sister in Dallas and had to come home a day early. He'd put a lot of thought into how to tell his mother and decided that the truth would break her heart—she and his father had enjoyed a strong, loving marriage, and the last thing she'd want for her one of her boys was a loveless union. So he'd stretched the truth a little and told her that he'd been seeing Harper for months and left out any reference to the fact they were embarking on a marriage of convenience. Even though his mother had admitted to some surprise, she'd clearly interpreted the story as a whirlwind romance and was thrilled about both the wedding and the babies.

She patted his tie. "Of course I came. I had to meet the woman crazy enough to marry you."

"Jesus, Mom," Nick said and shot a glance at Harper. His mother and brother's humor didn't always translate well to strangers, but thankfully Harper was chuckling. He shook his head. "So much for family support."

"It's okay, honey," his mother said. "Harper and I have had a few moments to chat. I like her. And your father, bless his soul, would have liked her, too."

Nick lifted a fist to his heart to push against the pressure that always came with the mention of his father. It had been nine years since he'd died, and they all still missed him like crazy. But today the grief was complicated by something else as well—by his mother giving a blessing on behalf of his dad. It was bad enough lying to one parent, but he felt like he was deceiving both of them now.

He managed to hold back the flinch and hoped any reaction she saw would be attributed to simply missing his father on his wedding day. He found a smile and said, "Thanks, Mom."

"Now," she said, reverting to her teasing tone, "are those for me?" She pointed to the bouquet in his hand that he'd forgotten he was carrying.

Not bothering to reply to more ribbing, he handed them to Harper. "I wasn't sure if you were getting one, so I figured I'd pick this up just in case."

"Thank you. That was very sweet," she said and gently touched the petals of the cream and pale pink flowers. "They're beautiful."

She snapped off one cream rose and threaded the stem into the top buttonhole of his suit jacket. As she adjusted it, her tongue peeked out, the tip coming to rest against her top lip. His skin heated. If they weren't surrounded by people—including his mother and brother—he'd pull her close and kiss that lip. She glanced up when she finished and must have seen the thought in his eyes, because her breath hitched. He held back a groan—her reaction certainly wasn't going to help rein in his own response.

Straightening his spine, with his gaze on hers so she understood, he stepped back.

"You know," Malcolm whispered as Harper turned away to talk to their mother, "this act for Mom is so good even I'm starting to buy it."

"Don't get carried away by the sight of a bouquet and a celebrant."

"Don't get carried away? Hang on—you know this is a real, legally binding ceremony, right?"

"Harper and I have talked it through. We have no illusions about romance. We're doing what's right."

Malcolm raised an eyebrow. "Do the two things have to be mutually exclusive?"

"Just tell me you have the rings."

Malcolm grinned. "I have the rings. The rings that symbolize your commitment—mind, body and soul—to this woman."

Nick prayed for the strength not to murder his brother on his own wedding day and turned to talk to his mother and Harper.

Ten minutes later, they were shown into another room, where a waiting city official greeted them and checked that they had two witnesses, rings and the paperwork.

Nick glanced around. This simple, practical ceremony was nothing like his first wedding to his high school sweetheart. That had been a big, white wedding—more of a spectacle than anything. He'd been uncomfortable being the center of attention, but he would have done anything for Melissa back when he'd thought in terms of forevers and true loves.

And yet, despite its lack of trappings—or maybe because of it—there was something so very real about this ceremony. He gave himself a shake. He couldn't lose sight of the facts— this arrangement was strictly practical. A way to solve all the issues that had arisen from Harper's pregnancy and his custody case, nothing more.

The formalities were surprisingly short, which suited him because he didn't want to linger, and since neither of them had written their own vows, the rite was even more streamlined.

Then, when they exchanged rings, something shifted inside him. The slow, ritualized movement of their hands carried meaning, carried weight that he hadn't suspected. It was as if the air around them was thick, insulating them, holding them, drawing them closer. He'd told his brother that he wouldn't get carried away, and yet he was in danger of doing exactly that.

And, curiously, from the flicker of emotion in Harper's eyes, she wasn't unaffected by the act of placing her ring on his left hand and having his slide down her finger, either.

But the time passed quickly, and soon they were being congratulated—his mother hugging them both, Malcolm slapping him on the back and shaking his hand. Through it all Nick was torn between accepting the congratulations in the spirit they were offered and feeling bad about deceiving his mother. He settled on allowing himself to feel satisfied that the plan had come together.

"So," Malcolm said and checked his watch, "it's almost noon. How about we get some lunch to celebrate?"

"Great idea." His mother looped her elbow through Harper's as they all headed for the exit.

"Maybe another time. We're spending this afternoon moving Harper's things to my place."

"Need some help?" Malcolm asked.

The rest of the day with his twin in an obnoxiously

cheery mood, taking potshots at him? Not appealing.
Besides, Nick wanted some time alone with Harper to
start working out what their marriage would look like.

They stepped out onto the sidewalk in front of city
hall, and Nick took Harper's hand. "We'll be fine."

Malcolm tuned to their mother. "I think the love-
birds want to be alone."

She nodded sagely. "They only have a weekend
for the honeymoon, so it makes sense not to waste
today with us."

Despite the grain of truth in the teasing, Nick
didn't rise to the bait. "Thanks again for coming
along. It means a lot."

"It really does," Harper echoed.

"Our pleasure," his mother said, and kissed each
of them on the cheek. "But we can take a hint, can't
we, Malcolm?"

"Oh, I understood the hint. I was just planning on
ignoring it," Malcolm said cheerfully.

"Don't worry," their mother said, "we're going
now." She grabbed a protesting Malcolm's arm and
marched him toward the parking lot the way she had
when the twins were ten.

Harper laughed. "I like your mother."

"I'm glad," Nick said. He dug his free hand in his
pocket and let out a long breath. "So, we're married."

The look in her beautiful brown eyes seemed uncertain. "It appears we are."

A light breeze picked up a few strands of her hair
and blew them across her face, so he tucked them behind her ear. "Ready for the move?"

Her stomach rumbled, and she smiled ruefully. "As long as we can grab some food on the way."

"Deal," he said, glad for at least one task that didn't involve lying and where he could make everyone happy.

Four

When he pulled up in front of Harper's house, Nick switched off the engine and grabbed the Mexican takeout they'd bought on the way. Everything was happening so fast, from discovering he was going to be the father of twins, to the wedding today and now moving her things to his place. The adrenaline from the changes was leaving him restless, but hopefully once she moved in, things would slow down some and they could find their feet. They got along well and had chemistry to burn, so he was feeling optimistic this whole plan would work.

He followed Harper up the small pathway, and after she'd unlocked the front door, he put the food just inside, then scooped her up and carried her through.

She gasped, but gave a rueful laugh. "I think you're only supposed to carry the bride over the threshold of the marital home. We won't be living here, so there's no need."

"I don't want to tempt fate," he said, trying not to dwell on how good her weight felt in his arms. "This isn't a normal marriage—there's no point pretending otherwise. Yet we both have things riding on it, so I'm planning on doubling up on tradition and doing it at both places."

Her amusement slowly faded as the pulse at the base of her neck began to flutter, and he gave himself a moment to fully appreciate that he was holding her curves against his chest. He could feel the heat of her skin through her thin blouse, hear her breath catch in her throat.

"Nick…" she said, her voice unsteady. "We need to talk about…this. About…intimacy in our marriage."

He wanted to lift her a little higher in his arms, bring those pink lips up to meet his, to take his time and kiss her thoroughly, to learn how she liked to be kissed. And he could see from the heat in her eyes that she'd be right on board with that, despite her words. But if they did, they wouldn't stop. He knew that from experience. From the insistent beat in his blood. And he had a feeling from her tone that she wanted that discussion about intimacy first.

He put the brakes on every instinct he had and lowered her feet to the ground. The slide of her body lit his every nerve ending, and he had to close his eyes and grit his teeth until she stepped away.

When he opened his eyes again, she was adjusting her blouse and shaking her head as she looked down at the floor. "And maybe we should talk about it sooner rather than later."

"That sounds like a good idea," he admitted and tried to ignore his body still protesting at the distance between them.

"Just give me a minute to change. These aren't moving clothes," she said, waving a hand at the outfit she'd worn for their wedding. "If you want to get a start on lunch, there are plates in the cupboard above the counter."

He wasn't fooled as he watched her leave. Sure, she needed to change, but the timing was to give her a moment to compose herself. And, if he were honest, he could use the time, too. So, he imagined himself in a cold shower until he had his body back under his control.

She emerged a few minutes later, having changed into a soft lavender summer dress that set off her tan skin and swirled around her legs, and within moments he was right back needing a cold shower again.

He cleared his throat and held up the plates, cutlery and food. "I had a look around. The deck out back looks like a good spot for lunch."

She smiled, but it didn't reach her eyes. "That sounds lovely."

Once they were settled at her outdoor table with lunch on their plates, he leaned back in his seat. She didn't start eating; instead she pushed the food around her plate, clearly uncomfortable. So he gave her a hand and said, "You wanted to talk about where we stand on intimacy."

"Yes." She straightened her spine. "You said you were okay with consummating our marriage, but I'm not so sure."

It was what he'd expected she'd say, but still, he couldn't see why it would be a problem. "What are you worried will happen?"

She lifted one shoulder and let it drop. "We've talked about this being a practical arrangement, and that we'll be able to walk away after five years if we want. So, wouldn't the best thing be to keep those boundaries clear?"

That sounded sensible on the surface, but he had a feeling there was a deeper reason. "You think we'll fall in love if we sleep together again."

"Not necessarily fall in love," she said, her brows drawn together, "but maybe things would be...messier."

In general, he agreed—making love was a big step, and once you'd taken it, there was no going back. And yet... "We've already crossed that line. Is holding back now really going to help?"

She circled her throat with her delicate hand. "It's different now."

"Yeah, I know." He reached over and unwrapped her hand from her throat, then held it between his. "We've done this thing completely backward. Getting pregnant, then getting married, then getting to know each other."

"And I think adding intimacy in the middle of that

is almost like throwing a grenade in. It's volatile and unpredictable."

"Point taken." He wondered if she'd deliberately used military imagery to help him see her meaning. Either way, it had worked. "How about we focus on getting to know each other and then revisit the topic in the future."

"I'm happy to revisit it, but I can't see anything that will make me change my mind. If we want that clean break at the end, it might be safer to not cross the line again."

He wasn't sure if she was suggesting they both have lovers outside the marriage, or that they both be celibate for the five years—neither of which was a palatable option—but now wasn't the time to push it. The day they wed and moved in together already had enough intensity for any twenty-four-hour period.

"Noted," he said. "We'll revisit once we're more settled."

They chatted about simpler subjects as they ate, but there was one topic that was important and couldn't wait for another day.

He put his plate down and brushed off his hands. "Do you have plans for tomorrow?"

"I was going in to the office for a few hours." She picked up a stray chili and popped it in her mouth.

"Tomorrow is Saturday," he clarified in case she'd lost count of the days amid the wedding preparations. "Do you often go in on the weekends?"

She finished chewing and found another chili while she spoke. "Sometimes. Depends what I have on my plate. But I was planning on heading in tomorrow because I took time off today for the wedding."

His brows drew together. "Does Malcolm expect you to make that time up?"

"He hasn't said anything." She shrugged.

"I'm guessing not, since he was there, too."

"Ah, but he's the boss. Things are always different for those in power—they follow a different set of rules entirely. I can't afford to let things slide just because of a wedding ring."

"I think you're forgetting something." He gave her a cocky grin. "I own half the company, too."

"You're pulling the boss card?" she asked, her tone halfway between surprised and amused.

"Sure, why not?"

She shook her head. "That's not a free pass for me, Nick. If anything, it means I have to be more careful. Once they know, the rest of the staff will be watching, waiting for signs of favoritism. Everything will need to be business as usual at work—I wouldn't risk my reputation."

"Tell me this. Do you have time off saved up?"

"Some."

"Why do I get the feeling it's more than *some*?" he asked mildly.

"There's always more work to be done and never really a good time to take the hours off. Besides, I take pride in my job and like to see that the work gets done. That's more important than the number of hours in my contract."

"Is there anything on your desk that can't wait until Monday?"

She finished the last of her lunch and laid down her cutlery.

"Not technically."

He had a feeling that the real answer was not at all. That she'd made sure that anything urgent was already taken care of, just in case.

"Then I have an alternative plan." He paused and smiled. "I have Ellie tomorrow, and I want you to come with us."

Harper bit down on her bottom lip.

"Are you okay?" he asked, watching her closely.

"I know that one of the reasons we got married was to present the picture of a stable family unit to the outside world. And the only way to do that is for me to meet Ellie, and to let people—especially your ex-wife—see the family we're creating. I guess I just didn't expect it to be this soon. I thought I'd have time to prepare."

There was tension in her expression that she was trying to cover, so he took her hand again. "You don't need to prepare. Just be yourself and Ellie will love you."

Harper thought about it for a moment, then drew in a breath and gave him a tentative smile. "I'd love to spend the day with you and Ellie."

He nodded, feeling more satisfied that she was going to meet his daughter than he would have expected. And it felt like it was about more than just the plan, the groundwork for his claim to be able to provide a stable family environment for his custody case. A sense of unease began to creep over him, prodding him to consider the level of their entanglement already, but he pushed it away. This was simply his strategy to achieve all their goals. And it was going according to plan. Everything would be fine.

Harper stepped through the internal door from the staircase that connected the garage beneath Nick's home to the living room and looked around. He'd been right in his description—it was sleek and modern with lots of white. She'd expected that would mean cold and impersonal, yet the warm caramels and chocolate browns, polished wood floor and highlights in lush greens somehow made it feel more like a crisp, natural setting. And with all the trees visible through the windows, the room blended in with its surroundings. She smiled and a little of the tension left her shoulders. This was a place she could be comfortable.

"A quick tour?" Nick said from beside her. "Or do you need something from your suitcases right away?"

She hadn't brought much in the suitcases—work clothes, casual clothes, laptop, bathroom items and a few extras. Her place wasn't that far to go back and grab things as she needed them. And keeping the connection to her house meant she still had a place that was all hers if things went wrong with Nick. She winced, uneasily aware that it could look as though she wasn't one hundred percent committed to the marriage by leaving herself an escape route, but, as

Nick had pointed out, this was a practical arrangement. She was just being practical about the possibility it wouldn't work.

She draped the clothes she'd brought on hangers over the back of the huge plush sofa and straightened. "I'll take the tour, thanks."

"Good choice," he said. "Then you can start settling in. I'll bring your bags to your room when we're done."

She hitched her handbag a little higher on her shoulder as she followed him through an archway.

"Kitchen," he said as they moved into a room of gleaming silver appliances and stone counters, then headed into a hallway.

He pointed to a room to her right, said, "Main bathroom," and kept going. Farther down the hall, he waved his arm from one side to the other. "Two of the guest bedrooms."

She looked down a staircase beside the one that went to the garage. "Where do those stairs lead?"

"Home gym. You're welcome to use it anytime. And next to that is my Tate Armor office. Most of the place is on one level except for those rooms and the garage." He continued on, and she had a glimpse of a darkened room, equipped with lots of technology. "Media room," he said, but they passed too quickly for her to peek.

They reached the end of the hall, where it branched off to the left and right. "That goes to my rooms," he said, nodding to the right. "Down here, though," he said, guiding her along the left hallway, "is the guest wing, which is now yours."

A few steps down the hall was a large bedroom, decorated in pale green and cream, with a king-size bed taking center stage. Windows filled the wall on two sides, and through another door, she spied an en-suite bath and shower. Nick crossed the room to built-in cupboards that lined one wall and opened one to reveal drawers, shoe racks and space to hang garments. "If there's anything else you need in here, let me know."

The room was beautiful, but it didn't have the feel of her bedroom at her own house, where she'd lovingly chosen every element to create her own sanctuary. Perhaps this would come to feel that way with time…

"I can't think of anything," she said. "It all seems lovely. Thank you."

"There's another room through here," he said, striding over to a door on the far wall. "I thought we could use this as the nursery."

She followed him in and found a room painted in the same pale green and cream color scheme, empty but for two armchairs.

"It was a sitting room for the guest wing," he said. "I took the rest of the furniture out to make way for nursery furniture."

At his words, tears pressed at the backs of her eyes, and she laid a hand over her stomach. Her babies would share this room. Sleep here. Smile and laugh here. She'd read them stories in this room. "It's perfect," she said.

After a moment of heavy silence, Nick cleared his throat. "We'll need to go shopping for baby furniture and equipment."

She dug into her handbag for her cell and brought up a screen before handing it to him. "I made a list."

He raised an eyebrow as he took the phone. "Already?"

"I like to be prepared."

As she waited, she watched him scroll through the list. He had no expression while he was reading—he wasn't giving anything away. She fidgeted with her fingernails. Past boyfriends, and even friends, had chided her for being too obsessive with planning and lists. One had called her regimental. She hadn't taken it personally—mostly because being organized had been a huge advantage in her career. But suddenly she was gripped with an unfamiliar bout of nerves. It seemed that it mattered what Nick thought. A lot.

"What do you think?" she asked brightly when she couldn't wait another second. "You're the experienced one."

He looked up with wide eyes and a lopsided grin. "This is amazing. We weren't this organized for Ellie. We should start getting the stuff on this list soon."

She let out a long breath that she hadn't realized she'd been holding. He hadn't been put off by her detailed list. In fact, he seemed to see it as a positive. She smiled. "That would be great."

He handed the cell back. "Any thoughts about names?"

"I looked at a few websites, but I was overwhelmed." Most of the time, she was still having trouble imagining herself with two children, let alone what their names would be.

"That's okay," he said, digging a hand into his pocket. "There's plenty of time."

"What about you?"

"I've always liked old-fashioned names—Eloise was my contribution to the name list—but we can decide together when you've had a chance to think about it."

She wandered over to the armchairs and trailed her fingers along the soft fabric.

"What about work?" Nick asked. "Do you see yourself working through the pregnancy?"

She turned back to him and wrapped her hand around the nape of her neck. "Good question. I haven't had a lot of time to think about it, because my original plan had been leaving Tate Armor and heading home to Connecticut. I thought I'd look for some consulting work there that I could do from home."

"And now that you're staying?" he said, leaning back against the wall and digging his hands into his pockets.

"I guess I'd like to keep working while I can. I'm not sure how I'll feel during the pregnancy, so it's hard to know." There were so many unknowns at the moment that could overwhelm her if she let them. She was definitely in favor of not letting them.

"One thing Tate Armor has given me is a very healthy bank balance. So if you decide you want to take a year off, or whatever, we have the financial freedom to do that."

Without warning, her throat constricted with emotion, and she couldn't speak. It wasn't about the money—though that was nice. It was him talking about them as a team. *We have the financial freedom.* It had been so long since someone other than her mother had said they had her back, or was willing to make contingency plans around her needs. It felt so very *nice*.

Nick must have noticed her expression change, because he pushed off the wall and crossed to take her hand. "Are you all right?"

"I'm good." She smiled at him. "I just like the idea of us being a team and facing the world together."

"I like that, too," he said and rubbed his thumb against her palm.

She opened her mouth to say more, but hesitated. There was a danger here. They'd made this plan and committed to it, but she couldn't allow herself the luxury of coming to depend on him. Real partnerships were the ones that were built on a foundation of trust and knowing each other. Those had the potential to stand the test of time. Her relationship with Nick was too new to know anything for sure.

And she couldn't risk being lulled into a false sense of security.

Five

Nick switched off the engine, and they sat in his ex-wife's driveway for a moment in silence.

"Do you want me to wait here?" Harper asked.

Given that Melissa always seemed to be on the offensive, having Harper wait in the car would be the path of least resistance. But that wouldn't achieve the effect he wanted. He needed the appearance of a family unit. It was the first step in his new campaign for shared custody of Ellie.

He reached over and squeezed Harper's hand. "We'll start as we mean to go on."

They walked along the pathway hand in hand, but before he could knock, the door swung open and he was confronted with the woman he'd once thought was the love of his life. And she wasn't happy.

Gripping the door handle tightly in one hand, and pointing at Harper with the other, Melissa wore an expression of pure accusation. Without bothering with a greeting, she said, "No girlfriends. We've talked about this. It creates an unstable environment for Ellie when they change."

Melissa's scumbag fiancé, Guy Hansen, appeared behind her, his half smile all affability, but it was a thin veil covering the menace in his eyes. "I'm afraid that's a nonnegotiable. No girlfriends around Ellie. I know we're all worried about Ellie's best interests."

Nick felt his blood pressure rise. Who was this man to lecture him about his own daughter's best interests? He drew in a steadying breath and smiled even more broadly than the other man.

"No need to worry. Harper isn't my girlfriend. She's my wife." He held up their joined hands to show Harper's wedding ring, then his other hand to display his

Melissa gasped. "You're *married*?"

The sleazy fiancé put an arm around Melissa's shoulders and gave him a stern look. "Now, Nick, this joke is in poor taste. You know how seriously Melissa takes things when it comes to Ellie."

Nick gritted his teeth and ignored the unspoken accusation of the statement—that he didn't take his daughter seriously enough—and instead pulled his eyebrows together in mock confusion. "Legally binding marriage vows are no laughing matter, Guy."

Melissa's expression morphed from disbelief to suspicion. "You weren't even seeing anyone."

"It's been a while since we knew each other's movements, Melissa," he drawled with a hint of a smile. "We're divorced, remember?"

Guy bristled and drew Melissa even closer against his side. "You're just doing this for the custody case."

He felt Harper stir beside him, ready to come to his defense, but he squeezed her hand, silently letting her know that he was fine. "Now, why would I need any help with the custody case?"

Guy opened his mouth, but Melissa cut him off. "How did you two meet?"

Easy. "Harper is an attorney for Tate Armor."

Melissa's eyes narrowed. "Are you trying to tell me that you're hands-on with the business now?"

"Actually, I'm not trying to tell you anything. As I pointed out, we're divorced. Now, I'd like to see my daughter."

Melissa met his gaze and held it, clearly deciding whether it was worth trying to satisfy her curiosity further or not…and gauging the likelihood of him telling her more. He didn't blink.

Then she called over her shoulder, "Ellie. Sweetheart, your father is here."

Seconds later, his daughter came tumbling from the living room in a red-and-white polka-dot dress, arms outstretched, calling, "Daddeee!" He scooped her up, gave her a loud, smacking kiss on the cheek and held her tight. As he breathed in her sweet scent, the world was suddenly a better place.

Harper listened to Nick and Ellie chat in the car

for the entire trip to the park. She was impressed by Nick's patience as the little girl jumped from topic to topic. From what Ellie had for breakfast—pancakes. To science questions—how do birds fly? To sightings of her favorite color car   yellow.

Given how reluctant Nick had been to make small talk with his mother and brother, Harper was pleasantly surprised at how easily he seemed to engage in chatty and convoluted conversations with Ellie. Of course, Ellie was adorable and clearly idolized him, which would make her a much more charming partner in discussion than a brother who seemed to delight in trying to get a rise out of him.

When they pulled up and Nick unbuckled Ellie from her child restraint, Harper decided it was time to join in. Developing a relationship with Ellie was an important part of being able to make a good impression on the judge, but more than that, Ellie would be the big sister to the babies. That sibling bond would be priceless, and Harper wanted to start building bridges between them now. Which meant she needed to forge a relationship with Ellie herself.

They wandered over the crisp green grass, the angelically beautiful Ellie holding Nick's hand, and Harper casting around for something to say. Then she saw a group of older kids at the other end of the park flying brightly colored kites.

"Ellie," she began in a chirpy voice, "would you like to go and see those kites?"

Ellie glanced up at the sky, her long, ice-blond hair dancing in the breeze, one hand shading her eyes.

"No, thank you," she said politely, then went back to chatting with her father.

Nick threw Harper a rueful smile, then said, "How about we head for the swings?"

Ellie leaped a step and flashed her enchanting smile. "Yes!"

"I love swings," Harper said. In fact, swings made a whole heap of sense—they were more interactive and fun than watching other kids playing, which was all that would have happened with the kites. She mentally filed the information away for future reference.

Once they reached the swing set, Nick lifted Ellie into a swing and Harper tried again.

"Would you like me to push you?" she asked.

Ellie twisted around to see her, her gray-green eyes earnest. "Can Daddy do it?"

It was a totally reasonable request from a little girl who loved her father, so despite a small pang of disappointment, Harper couldn't begrudge her wanting Nick.

"Of course," she said and stepped back.

Once Nick had a squealing Ellie swinging in rhythm, he glanced over at Harper. "You okay?"

"Sure." She focused on Ellie's utter delight in soaring through the air, her hair flying behind her. "I guess I didn't think it would be this hard."

"It's only because she doesn't see me often enough," he said, as if that was all there was to it. And maybe it was, but deep down, Harper suspected it was more.

"It's just that if I can't get a three-year-old to let me push her on a swing, it doesn't bode well for parenting two babies." Her stomach dipped as she said the words aloud. This was why her first plan once she'd known she was pregnant had been to move home and get help from someone experienced with children.

He pushed the swing and turned to her. "You'll be a great mother, Harper. Are you having doubts?"

"About that, and pretty much everything," she conceded.

He arched an eyebrow. "About us?"

"Actually, this has shown me that you're the person I need to help with the babies." If he could inspire love and devotion in a child he didn't get to see often enough, then he'd be a beautiful father for their twins.

"*We'll* be great," he said, his focus intense. "Together."

It meant a lot that she had his support, especially when she was doubting herself. She smiled at him. "Thanks."

"Right," he said more loudly. "Who's ready for the best snack in the state of Texas?"

"Me!" Ellie said from high in the air.

It was a fairly quick trip to the Royal Diner, a journey once again filled with father-daughter chatter. The diner, with its '50s style decor and informal atmosphere, was popular, but they managed to squeeze in and were soon settled in a red faux-leather booth with menus.

A tall man in uniform stopped by and greeted Nick. Harper recognized him as Sheriff Nathan Battle. They might not have met before, but she'd seen him on TV. After shaking the man's hand, Nick introduced Harper to him as his wife. The sheriff never missed a beat, but his eyes widened.

"Good to meet you," he said and stuck out his hand.

She took his hand and shook it. "You, too, Sheriff Battle."

He turned back to Nick. "Don't suppose you've heard any whispers about anyone being targeted by Maverick?"

Nick shot her a look, and Harper was relieved all over again that they'd managed to marry before Maverick had gotten wind of their situation and caused trouble.

"Not a word," Nick said. "Wouldn't you be the first to hear?"

Sheriff Battle shook his head. "Some of the information Maverick has been digging up has been…of a sensitive nature, so if he has a new victim, there's no guarantee the victim will want law enforcement involved."

"I'll keep an ear out and let you know if I hear anything."

"I'd appreciate that," the sheriff said and turned to go. "By the way, you should try the curly fries. I might be biased, but Amanda Battle makes the best curly fries in the state."

Nick laughed. "Will do, Sheriff."

After the other man left, Nick glanced across the table, his daughter by his side and his eyes full of mischief. "I know what Ellie wants."

It was clearly a game and he was including her,

and Harper felt a rush of gratitude. "What does Ellie want?" she said, playing along.

"Ellie wants…a tall glass of pineapple juice."

The words were barely out of his mouth before Ellie said, "No!" and giggled.

Harper grinned. "You know, Nick, I'm not sure she wants pineapple juice."

He held up an index finger, as though he'd remembered something. "Then I know what she *does* want."

"Oh, yeah?" Harper made an exaggerated serious face. "What's that?"

Nick threw his hands out as if making a big announcement. "Iced tea. With lots of ice cubes."

"No, Daddy," Ellie responded, giggling louder. "I want—"

But Nick cut her off. "No, no, don't tell me. Because I know she really wants a nice, big, cold glass of tomato juice."

"No!" Ellie practically squealed in between laughs.

Nick looked down at his daughter, confused, then over to Harper. "That's strange, because I thought they were her favorite things."

"Milk shake," Ellie said, in between gasps of laughter.

"Oh, right. A milk shake. Now I remember. But," he said conspiratorially to Harper, "she doesn't like them thick. The runnier the better for our Ellie."

Ellie fell into fits of giggles again. "No!"

"No? Not runny?" When his daughter shook her head in wide sweeps, he shrugged. "Okay, when the waitress comes, I'll order a double-thick milk shake for you."

"Triple!"

"Triple?" he said, running a hand over his chin. "I'm not sure you can handle a triple-thick milk shake."

"I can, Daddy!" She grabbed at his hand, as if that would reinforce her point. "I can!"

He picked up a menu and scanned it as he spoke, his tone suggesting it was the end of the matter. "All right. A triple-thick watermelon-flavored milk shake."

"Banana!"

Finally, Nick burst into laughter. "Okay," he said, looping an arm around Ellie's shoulders and pulling her into his side. "Banana. And a bowl of curly fries. When the sheriff of the town tells us to try his wife's curly fries, we'd best take heed."

"Yay! I love you, Daddy." She reached her little arms up, pulled his head down and planted a kiss on his cheek. For a fleeting moment, there was an expression of pure, unadulterated happiness on Nick's face.

If there had ever been any doubt that his daughter meant the world to him, that look proved it without a shadow of a doubt.

The waitress came and took their orders—Ellie ordered her own milk shake, just to be safe—and Harper glanced over the menu. Her morning sickness hadn't been too bad, but she wasn't going to be able to stomach a triple-thick milk shake and greasy fries, so she ordered some plain toast and tea.

"Feeling okay?" Nick asked when the waitress left.

She nodded. "I'm fine. I just couldn't handle all that rich food."

Nick clearly didn't want to ask about morning sickness in front of his daughter. He gave Harper a reassuring smile and started chatting with Ellie again. Which was the exact strategy Harper wanted to take as well—leave the grown-up stuff until later, and have another go at bonding with Nick's little girl.

But what did three-year-olds talk about? She couldn't ask Ellie what her career plans were, or if she'd tried the new restaurant in town. And all she knew about the little girl was that she loved her dad, swings and triple thick-milk shakes, none of which provided a new topic of conversation.

She glanced over at Nick's daughter, looking for clues. She wore a bright red dress with white polka dots. Perhaps she'd chosen it this morning and especially liked the colors or pattern? It was worth a try.

When there was a break in conversation on the other side of the table, Harper said, "Ellie, that's a lovely dress you're wearing."

The little girl smiled. "Thank you, ma'am."

Ma'am? Harper cringed inside. God, she was going backward.

Nick dropped a quick kiss on the top of his daughter's head. "You can call her Harper."

"Okay," Ellie said, but she didn't repeat the name.

Once again Harper cast around for something to talk about and then noticed a little fluffy toy wedged on the bench seat between Ellie and her dad. It seemed to be an animal.

"Who's that?" she asked, pointing at the toy.

Ellie pulled it out and tucked it up under her chin. "Annabel."

Now that Harper could see it better, she made out that it was a stuffed dog. Harper practically sighed in relief—finally a topic she knew something about.

"I love dogs," she said brightly.

Clearly having experience with insincere adults, Ellie looked skeptical, so Harper explained more. "I always had a dog growing up. There was Marshall the Great Dane, and Darcy the Labrador. Do you know what type of dog Annabel is?"

"A beagle," Ellie said, her expression a little less suspicious now.

"Oh, I love beagles, but I've never met one before. Will you introduce me to Annabel?"

Ellie looked down at her little dog then whispered in its ear. She waited, as if listening, then looked back up at Harper.

"Annabel, this is Daddy's friend Harper. Harper, this is my Annabel." She held the toy across the table, but her grip said she wasn't letting go.

Harper reached out and shook one of the little paws. "Lovely to meet you, Annabel. I hope we can become friends, too."

Ellie put the dog up to her ear and nodded during the imaginary conversation, then turned back to Harper. "Annabel says okay. You can be friends."

Harper's heart lifted. It might only have been a small step—one with a stuffed toy, at that—but it was a step, and she'd take all she could get.

"Thank you, Annabel. I'd like that a lot."

The waitress returned, bringing their food, and the conversation returned to center on the banter between father and daughter, but Harper didn't mind. That small step of Ellie letting her toy dog be friends with her was enough to make her day.

As Nick bit into a bunch of fries, he met Harper's gaze and grinned broadly. The shared moment of triumph was almost like a window into the future—where they might end up as they jointly parented the twins, and further, as their babies grew into children.

And it felt good.

That night, they grabbed some Chinese takeout on the way home and ate it while watching a movie. Nick was feeling pretty good about life. He'd spent the day with his little girl, and now he was on the sofa with Harper.

She'd tried so hard today to form a relationship with Ellie—and it had been more than just for appearances' sake, he felt that deep in his bones. She'd *wanted* to create a bond with his daughter. His heart had swelled as he'd watched them talking at the diner. But he was feeling something completely different now when he looked at Harper...

The TV was on, playing a show he normally watched, but he couldn't follow the storyline. Not with Harper's body mere inches away. The occasional brush of her leg against his as she leaned forward to pick up her drink from the coffee table set every nerve on edge; the smell of her floral shampoo curled through his senses.

But she'd made it clear she didn't want the complications that would arise from taking their intimacy any further, so he really needed to distract himself.

"Do you want dessert?"

"I'm not normally a big dessert eater, but maybe I could tonight." She placed a hand on her stomach. "These babies must be hungry."

"I'm not surprised they're hungry. We Tates have big appetites."

She laughed. "Go on, then. What options do you have?"

"There's fruit in the bowl on the counter."

"Nope," she said. "That won't satisfy these two. What else?"

He ran through the options in his mind. "I'm pretty sure there's ice cream in the freezer."

"Now that's more promising. What flavor?"

"To be honest, I don't remember."

"Are you serious? You have ice cream in the house and you haven't paid enough attention to it to know what type it is?"

"It doesn't matter that much, does it? It's all ice cream."

She pressed a hand to her chest, as if aghast, but her eyes were twinkling. "The flavor is *everything*."

He burst out laughing. She was laying it on thick, but she clearly cared about ice cream a hell of a lot more than he did. "Should we go and check?"

"I think we should."

He stood and held out a hand. She put her smooth palm on his, and he wrapped his fingers around it and pulled her to her feet. For several heartbeats, he didn't move, just held her hand, standing a little too close. His body heated, and her eyes widened a fraction, but before he could do something stupid like kiss her, he remembered that the purpose of offering dessert was to distract himself from wanting her.

He released her hand and stepped back. "I can guarantee one thing," he said, trying for and luckily finding a light tone. "It's not mint ice cream."

"You don't like mint?" she asked, clearly trying to match his tone.

"Sure I do. In toothpaste. Why would I want toothpaste-flavored ice cream?"

She shrugged. "Point taken."

They reached the freezer, and he pulled out an unopened tub and read the label. "Peanut butter with caramel swirl."

She frowned, so he held up the container for her to see.

"You're a man of surprises, Nick Tate."

"What were you expecting?" he practically drawled.

"I'm not sure. Maybe coffee, maybe dark chocolate. But not—" she looked down at the label "—peanut butter with a caramel swirl."

He kept a poker face, but he liked this playful version of Harper. "Don't knock something until you've tried it." He pulled open the cutlery drawer and grabbed a spoon. "You're going to be singing my praises in a few minutes."

"Is that so?" She grinned, her brown eyes dancing.

After removing the lid, he scooped out a small spoonful and held it out to her. Harper leaned in. Her lips closed over the ice cream and pressed firmly together. His pulse spiked, and he realized the flaw in his plan. Dessert was meant to distract him from his wanting, not increase it.

He clenched his jaw and tried to suppress every scrap of desire that hummed through his blood.

Then she moaned, and her eyes drifted shut. "That. Is. Sinful," she murmured.

Her eyes opened again, and he focused on the spoon in his hand. On autopilot, he dug out another bite-size scoop and fed it to her. This time, she leaned forward to meet him partway, and as she opened her mouth in readiness, he glimpsed her pink tongue and damn near groaned himself.

Her eyes closed again, and the look of bliss that stole over her face almost did him in.

"Harper," he rasped.

Her eyes flew open, and the want, the need in her gaze were as strong as ever, but she was looking at him instead of the ice cream.

He was a goner.

Harper watched Nick and tried to keep her breathing under control. Being so close to him on the sofa as she'd pretended to watch TV had set every single nerve ending she had on edge. And then he'd fed her ice cream… Her skin yearned for his touch, but if she gave in now, all would be lost—she might not be able to pull back.

Then she noticed the strong, insistent beat of his pulse at the base of his neck. The tension in his muscles as he held himself in check. The way his gaze smoldered.

And she forgot what they were fighting against.

"Nick?" she asked, her voice breathless.

"Yeah?"

"What would happen if we gave in?"

His gaze flicked to her mouth then back to her eyes. "Gave in to what?"

"To this." She motioned back and forth with a finger. "To what's burning between us."

He swallowed hard. "You really want to know?"

"Yeah, I do," she whispered.

He looked down at her in the dim light of the kitchen, then lowered his head until his lips brushed over hers, just once. "This."

A sigh built within her and escaped her throat as she leaned into him. "Oh. This is a good plan."

She lifted herself on tiptoes and found his mouth, warm and dark and inviting. He wrapped one arm around her waist, hauling her flush against him, and sank into the kiss she offered. The sizzling impact of his tongue, the decadence of it, had her whispering his name against his lips.

He pivoted and pushed her against the wall, pinning her with his weight as he kissed her like he hungered for her. Like she was the only thing necessary for life.

Panting, she wrenched her mouth from his. "I vote we stop fighting it for tonight," she said, then paused to catch her breath. "Just give ourselves this one night."

He leaned his forehead against hers, his breathing labored, too. "You have my vote."

"Okay, then. Well, if we're agreed—" she stepped away, leaving their laced fingers as their only connection "—this time we should aim for a bed."

One corner of his mouth hitched, and he headed off down the hall. She followed as he led her to his room. She hadn't been this way before, but she only barely noticed her surroundings—all her attention was on the man beside her.

He stepped into an open doorway and hit a switch with his fist. Soft light diffused through a large room dominated by a king-size bed. There were closed blinds on three sides, though small windows up high allowed fresh air in, and through another door, she spied an en-suite bath and shower that looked similar to hers. But now was not the time to explore. Now was the time for Nick.

"One more thing," he said and disappeared into the attached bathroom, returning seconds later with a little packet of protection.

She grinned. "I'm already pregnant."

"I'm clean, but I want you to know for sure."

"I'm clean, too, but thank you." She stepped closer. "So, I guess dessert is out of the question?"

"There's no more ice cream." He kissed her softly

before saying against her mouth, "But I've been dreaming of tasting every square inch of you."

Spearing fingers into her hair, he cradled her head as he kissed her—taking exquisite care with ravishing her mouth. It wasn't enough. Would never be enough. With hands flat on his chest, she gently pushed, needing the room to explore his body, and he took the hint. Clothes were in the way, but still, she took advantage of the opportunity and roamed her hands across his broad shoulders, down his arms, across his chest, acclimatizing herself to him again. And he stood still, allowing her the freedom to do what she wished.

"My turn," he said, his gaze burning. She wasn't nearly finished, but it was fair, so she dropped her hands and waited to see what he'd do.

Button by excruciating button, he unfastened the front of her summer dress and pushed the sides open, exposing her skin to the cool night air. Her pulse fluttered madly. In simple movements, he unhooked her bra and let it drop to the floor, and she felt her breasts tighten in the light breeze from the high windows— and under his all-consuming gaze.

"Harper," he said and swallowed hard. "You're so damned beautiful."

She didn't answer. Couldn't. So instead she reached for him again and focused on touching him, on feeling him touch her.

His hands sliding down her sides, across her stomach, felt like fire licking at her skin. In idle moments she'd wondered if their electric connection that first night had been because of its illicit nature, and whether making love with him now that he was her husband would have less of an edge. Less intensity. Now she had her answer. He…they…*this* was so much more than anything she'd experienced before. More than she'd imagined.

She pulled at his shirt where it was tucked into his trousers. Then, not bothering with the buttons, she tugged it over his head. His skin was beautiful, so beautiful, and the scars and marks that showed his history of putting his body on the line for others only made it more beautiful. The muscle definition on his abs was crazy—he'd obviously kept up whatever training the SEALs had him doing—and the crisp hair scattered across his chest called to her fingers. As she walked her fingertips over the dark hair, he shivered, and she smiled, glad she wasn't the only one affected this badly.

He captured her mouth. Not breaking the searing kiss, he took a step backward, taking her with him, then another, until they reached the edge of the bed. He finally released her mouth, grinned wickedly and fell backward onto the mattress, bringing her down on top of him.

The sensuous slide of their bodies set every nerve ending she had alight, but it wasn't enough. She reached for his belt, wanting all the fabric separating them gone, but he stayed her hand.

"Not yet," he said, his voice unsteady.

She could feel the blood pump through her body, strong and insistent. "I want more, now."

"No can do," he said as his thumb grazed the curve of her breast.

A delicious shiver raced over her skin, and she had to wait a moment for it to pass before she could speak again. "Why the holdup?"

"I want this to take all night." He hooked his fingers in the scraps of fabric around her hips and dragged them down over her legs before letting her underwear follow her bra over the side of the bed to the floor. "We have a lot to make up for."

"What do you mean?" she asked, starting to lose her train of thought.

"The night of the ball, our first time, it was rushed." He kissed a trail down the inside of her arm to her wrist, his hair tickling her ribs as he went.

She gasped, then found her breath again to reply. "I thought it was excellent."

Grinning, he caressed a pattern on her stomach. "Phenomenal."

"Then what's the problem?" She slid her leg up his thigh and hooked it around him, locking his hips against hers. What a shame he was being reluctant about removing his trousers...

"Now that we have more time," he said, rocking against her in defiance of his words, "I want to take it slow. To do all the things we didn't get around to."

He kissed her again, and while his mouth was busy, she unzipped his trousers and pushed them— and his boxers—as far down his legs as she could reach. Then she broke the kiss to remove them all the way before smiling back up at him. "See, it's all about your perspective."

He dipped his hand down until it slid between her legs, moving in patterns and with a rhythm that was going to drive her crazy. The way one corner of his mouth hooked up as he spoke told her he knew the effect he was having. "What other way is there to look at it?"

Her eyes drifted closed, but even if she couldn't see him, she could feel him everywhere. "You want this to be different from last time."

"I do," he said, his voice husky as his hand still moved to the melody of silent music.

"See, I'm thinking that's too prescriptive—" she paused to moisten her lips so her mouth could form the words "—for making love."

His hand stilled, and she opened her eyes to see him. His gaze was squarely on her, his brow creased as if he was trying to discern where she was going with this. "What do you have in mind?"

"That we stop thinking and just let it happen." There was something about his skin that she couldn't get enough of. Its texture, its scent. She dipped her tongue to sample the skin just above his collarbone, and dug her fingernails into his back. Dug them in and dragged them lightly across his shoulder blades. She could touch this man forever.

"I like your idea…really like it—" he drew in a quick breath and swallowed hard "—but I still want to take it slow."

Deciding the time for talking—for negotiating—

was over, she found the foil packet on the bedside table and quickly sheathed him before pushing at his shoulder until he rolled onto his back. She rose up over him and hesitated. The sight of him lain out on the bed, for her, the perfection of him, was overwhelming. He reached out, found her hand and linked their fingers palm to palm. It was exactly what she needed, securing her in the moment, grounding her. Then she sank down onto him, and, as their bodies connected, he let out a guttural groan.

She moved, drunk with desire, and he matched her rhythm, so they danced together as one. She was flying, free—the only things that mattered were Nick and the pleasure that was engulfing her.

He hooked his hands behind her knees and held them, anchoring her, changing the angle, and wave after wave of blinding heat consumed her as she imploded. While aftershocks still assailed her body, Nick called her name and a fierce shudder ripped through him.

Breathing ragged, she slid down to lie beside him, a possessive hand across his stomach, and he looped an arm around her shoulders. Cocooned with him, by him, her world slowly returned to normal, and she drifted off to sleep.

Six

Harper woke with a jolt, her heart in her mouth. The first thing she was aware of was shouting. The room was dark except for glimmers of moonlight through the blinds, which was enough to show unfamiliar surroundings, and the man beside her.

Nick.

His shouting eased to incoherent mumbling. Despite still being deeply asleep, his head moved with jerky rhythms and his hands seemed to punctuate his words.

Should she wake him? This was no happy dream—he was far too agitated for that to be possible—but wasn't there a rule about not waking someone from a nightmare? Or was that sleepwalking? She bit down on her bottom lip, wishing she'd paid more attention to wherever she'd heard the advice.

"No," he barked, eyes still closed as his hand sliced through the air. His wedding ring glinted in the moonlight, and it struck her anew that the man in her bed was her husband.

Husband.

They were married, and she knew less about him than about many of her coworkers. A wave of panic washed over her. She didn't really know this man, and she certainly didn't know how to help him now.

He shouted again, louder this time, then he screamed. It was a raw, guttural sound, full of pain and anguish, like nothing she'd ever heard before, and it sent cold prickles racing across her skin. She had to act.

Not wanting to wake him suddenly, she began to talk softly, soothingly, gradually raising her volume. The way his face contorted into expressions of utter despair broke her heart. In that moment, she wanted nothing more than to wrap him in her arms and take his pain away, but all she could do was keep up the litany of soothing words. Slowly, steadily, she talked him around. His screams died to tearless sobs, and she raised her voice again, to just above normal speaking volume. He drew in a deep, shaky breath, and as he released it, his eyes opened.

For a millisecond, the pain she'd witnessed was reflected in their depths until his eyes focused on her. She saw the moment he realized what had happened—just before the shutters came down. Hard.

He jumped out of bed and stood on the rug, skin covered in a sheen of perspiration, muscles clenched, his pose rigid, every inch of him proclaiming his military past. Despite being naked now, he'd been more exposed when he'd been asleep and covered by the sheet.

"Harper, I'm sorry," he said, his voice rough yet controlled.

"It was a nightmare." Smiling, she shook her head, wanting him to know everything was okay. "You have nothing—"

Expression flat, he cut her off. "You shouldn't have had to experience that."

Her heart broke a little for him then. He shouldn't have had to experience that, either. "It's okay, Nick, really—"

"I'll take a guest room." Without making eye contact, he reached for his phone and wristwatch from the bedside table, turned and walked through the door.

Stunned, she watched him go.

He was *leaving* her.

As he disappeared into the dark hallway, she had trouble filling her lungs. He might be virtually a stranger, but he was her husband, the man she'd made love with only hours ago. And now he was leaving the bed where they'd shared that passion.

A small, hard knot of panic sitting in the middle of her chest grew, enveloped her and bestowed the familiar taste of abandonment.

She tried logic, always her first line of defense— he'd left because he was still upset about the nightmare, not because of her. But it didn't ease the sour taste at the back of her mouth. She'd offered to be there for him while he dealt with the nightmare, so, yeah, he'd walked out on her.

Logic rarely worked when she was dealing with the slap of rejection, and she usually moved right on to the second line of defense—comfort eating. But she wasn't in her own home, and having to riffle through his kitchen cupboards for carbs and sugar would probably cancel out any comfort effects. Besides, she was trying to eat healthy for the babies.

So that left her with two options—curl up in a ball and let the emotion overwhelm her, or...

Or find Nick and get him to talk his nightmare through, both for his sake and so she could let go of the image of him walking out the door the way so many people in her life had done before him.

She stood and rubbed her hands over her face. This night had shown her one thing—she'd been right to think that sleeping together would make their relationship messy. They already had so many challenges in making their arrangement work, making love had been foolhardy. They'd risked their tentative cohesion merely for physical desires.

They couldn't afford to take the risk again.

But she couldn't dwell on that right now. First, she needed to deal with the fallout of this time and make sure Nick was okay.

Nick flicked the light on in the guest bedroom's bathroom and headed for the shower, trying to forget the look of horror on Harper's face. A look that had the power to haunt him forever.

That wasn't the expression he'd planned to leave on his new bride's face the first time he'd taken her to his bed…

He stepped under the hot spray of water and rested his palms on the wall behind the faucet, dipping his head to bear the full force of the spray.

Hell.

He should have known. Should have expected he couldn't just walk into a marriage the way a normal man could. Especially a marriage of convenience like this, where they were plunged into it with barely any emotional preparation. He'd been shot at and felt shells detonate close enough to make his teeth rattle too many times to count. He was partially deaf due to an explosion that had blown to bits some of the fiercest warriors he'd ever had the privilege to fight alongside. He'd been captured and held prisoner by a faction of rebels notorious for their treatment of prisoners. After all he'd been through, after all the damage to his soul, what made him think he could have special things in his life?

Like a marriage.

Like Harper.

He elbowed the tap and the water abruptly ceased, but he didn't immediately reach for the towel, letting the water drip from his body instead.

He'd have to find a way to apologize to her, to try to make this up to her—if that were even possible.

But not tonight, not while he was raw from both the nightmare and waking to see the trauma in her eyes.

He grabbed a towel and roughly rubbed it over his skin until it was dry, and if he was a little overzealous and left red marks, then all the better. Soft and gentle weren't things he deserved. Not when he'd come out alive and better men had come home in body bags.

Wrapping the towel around his hips, he headed through the door that connected the bathroom to the guest bedroom and stopped short when he saw Harper sitting on the edge of the bed in a fluffy blue robe tied firmly around her middle.

In the gentle light of the bedside lamp, she was so beautiful. Her back was straight, her chin jutting at a proud angle. She looked strong. Sure of her place in the world. Things he couldn't claim to be anymore. He glanced away.

"Harper, this is not the time."

She crossed her arms tightly under her breasts, clearly having no intention of going anywhere. "I think this is exactly the time. I have a feeling that if we leave this until morning, it will be even harder to discuss."

True enough, but he shook his head. "I'm not sure I can discuss it. It is what it is." Lord knew he'd tried hard enough to pretend otherwise.

"That may be, but we do need to talk," she said, her gaze on him unwavering. "Because this is not how I see our marriage working."

He planted his hands low on his hips. "It was just a nightmare, not our entire marriage."

"We entered into a marriage of convenience. There are already enough obstacles in our way without secrets. I think the only way we're going to make this whole thing work is if we have honesty and openness between us," she said, her voice steady, but her eyes asking—hoping for—so much of him.

"We're doing fine." The statement was so far from the truth that he was surprised she didn't laugh in his face.

But she didn't. Not his Harper. Instead she looked at him with eyes as deep as oceans, as raw and vulnerable as he'd ever seen in another person, and said, "I have to be honest. This feels an awful lot like being rejected on the same night we made love for the first time as a married couple."

That stung, deep in his chest. She'd told him about her past and her fear of abandonment, and he'd just played right into that fear and made it worse for her. Hell, someone needed to smack him upside the head.

"It's not you," he said, knowing the words were clichéd and inadequate. "It's me."

"Okay." She sat up straighter. "Then tell me about you."

He knew what she meant—tell her about the events that had led to the nightmares. And she was right—as his wife, she deserved to know—but he simply didn't know if he could say the words aloud. He rubbed his fingers across his forehead, then dug them into his temples.

"Nick, we have a difficult road ahead of us parenting two babies together, and we're both flying blind because we don't know much about each other." She reached for his hand, and he let her take it. "Tell me about this. Help me to understand."

He flinched. Flying blind—that's exactly what they were doing, and she deserved more. He sank down onto the bed beside her, his shoulders slightly hunched as he prepared to face the worst. For her.

"Nine—" Everything inside him clenched tight. He cleared his throat and started again. "Nine months ago, I came home from the Middle East. As far as everyone is concerned, I'm a decorated war hero."

"But you don't feel like one, do you?" she asked gently.

Yeah, understatement of the century. "The military might have given me a medal, but I've always known I didn't deserve it."

Her smile was kind. "I don't think they give those medals out for no reason."

"Men died while under my command," he said fiercely. A wave of nausea washed through him, and he pressed a closed fist to his gut to try to stem its progress. Those fine men were gone forever. Their families had lost sons. Children had lost parents. Wives had lost their husbands.

He stood and paced to the other side of the room, as if that could give him the distance he needed, even though he knew it wouldn't. Couldn't. He felt every one of those losses deeply. He saw their faces in his mind. He apologized to them every day, but it made no difference. It wouldn't bring them back.

Too damn little, too damn late.

"Oh, Nick."

He shook his head rapidly, trying to dispel the emotion from the story. He didn't want Harper's sympathy. He wasn't the one who deserved it.

He straightened his spine, squared his shoulders and told her the truth. "They gave me a medal because I was able to save most of my team, but it wasn't enough. That wasn't near enough. It was my responsibility to save them all."

"I'm sure you weren't solely responsible for those men's lives."

He squeezed his eyes closed tight against the memories. "I let them down."

There was silence for long moments until he opened his eyes again and found her watching him.

"It's torn you up inside, hasn't it?" she asked, her voice soft.

He met her gaze and almost smiled. Almost. "You could say I'm kind of a mess."

"Tell me," she said, and there was something in her tone that made him want to do just that. Wanted to share this with someone, and wanted that someone to be Harper, even though it might change her opinion of him forever.

"The doctors gave me painkillers for my wounds—" he paused to find the strength to admit the rest "—and I became addicted to them." To his eternal shame.

Her brows drew together. "I haven't seen you take anything."

She wouldn't have. Not now. He breathed in a lungful of air. At least this was one thing he could feel okay to admit. "I didn't want to be dependent on a chemical, so I did some treatment and learned to deal with the addiction."

"You're clean now?" she asked, her gaze steely.

"One hundred percent." He wouldn't have contemplated being part of Ellie's or the babies' lives if he wasn't. They were too precious.

Her gaze softened. "That takes a lot of strength."

"Oh, yeah?" He coughed out a laugh. "Did you notice the screaming nightmares?"

"I did," she said, with no judgment in her tone. "Tell me about them."

He leaned on the wall a few feet from her and slid to the carpet, wrists resting on his bent knees. "They started when I was in hospital, but they'd eased off a bit." He shrugged. "I didn't realize I was still having them."

Her head tilted to the side. "You don't remember them in the morning?"

Oh, he remembered them. Lord above, did he remember them. "I didn't realize I was yelling anymore." The thing was, he hadn't shared anyone's bed since the nightmares had started. Sure, he'd yelled during nightmares when he'd been recovering in the hospital after the last mission, but he'd assumed that phase was long over. It just went to show, he should never assume anything about his condition. "I swear, Harper, if I'd known that you'd be woken by them, that they'd affect you, I wouldn't have suggested we get married. I wouldn't have tied you to…this."

She dismissed that with a wave of her hand. "So, what do you want to do now?"

"What do you want?" he asked warily.

"I want us to make this marriage work for our children. We owe them that." Her eyes were intense. Certain.

"I'm as committed as ever to our vows—we're doing the right thing for the babies. I haven't been this sure about something in a long time."

"We're in agreement, then," she said and stood.

He gave one slow nod. "Next time we make love, it would be better for everyone if I left right after." The last thing any woman—especially a pregnant woman—needed was to be woken by someone in her bed screaming, and he simply wouldn't do that to her.

She crossed her arms under her breasts. "I don't think that's the right way forward for us."

He hauled himself to his feet and scrubbed his hands through his hair, wishing he had all the answers. "Harper, I saw you back there in that room. I won't be responsible for putting that expression of horror on your face again."

"I think we need to go back to our original plan. Bringing sexual intimacy into our relationship was a mistake."

He stepped closer and cradled the side of her face in his palm. "We can make it work, I promise. I just won't stay the night."

"Please don't make this harder than it is." She'd told him that her trigger was people walking away from her, and at the first test of their relationship, he'd done exactly that. He needed to take a step back, respect her boundaries and give her a chance to feel settled again.

"Are you sure that's what you want?"

"There's already so much pressure on this relationship. It can't be sexual as well." When he didn't reply, she added, "Nick?"

"Okay," he said reluctantly. He might not agree, but if she didn't want to, then there was no way forward for their physical relationship.

He took her hand and walked her back down the hall to her bedroom. In the doorway, he stopped. He wanted nothing more than to sink into that bed and pull Harper against him, but he couldn't. He laid a soft kiss on her lips, hoping she understood all that was still unsaid, and turned to go.

"Nick," she said.

He couldn't turn back. If he let his guard down for a single second, he'd join her in that bed. So, instead, he turned his head and spoke over his shoulder. "Yes?"

"Thank you."

She was *thanking* him? "For what?"

"For trusting me enough to share your past with me. I know that must have been hard, and I just want you to know I appreciate it."

Not sure of his voice, he nodded once and walked down the dark hall to his empty bed.

Harper opened her eyes the next morning to see Nick coming through the bedroom door holding a tray. She yawned and stretched, giving herself cover for a few moments to study him. The man before her was different from the one she'd sat with last night as he'd poured out his pain. This man had his mask firmly back in place. As someone who wore an invisible suit of armor to protect herself, she had no trouble recognizing his.

A stab of disappointment struck, as if she'd been given a gift that had been taken away again. But at the same time, part of her had to admire the skill and self-discipline it took to hide his pain from the world so well. It hadn't just been his words last night that had told her about the pain consuming him, it had been the soul-deep anguish in his eyes. Sharing that with her had been a huge act of trust. She wondered if he'd shared that with anyone before. Did Malcolm even know the depths of his torment?

"Morning," he said, giving her a smile that didn't reach his eyes.

She wriggled up in the bed so that she was sitting against the headboard, and he unfolded the legs on the tray and set it over her lap.

"Good morning," she said. The tray held a plate with two eggs on toast, a glass of juice and a small vase with a purple flower that looked to be from the bush beside the driveway that she'd seen last night. There might have only been a few items on the tray, but they were laid out in a neat and ordered way. She was still getting to know her husband, but this seemed to sum up his personality perfectly—he'd cared enough to cook her food, but kept it basic. He'd been sweet enough to cut a flower for her, then laid it all out with military precision. He was a study in opposites.

As he straightened, he rested his hands low on his hips. "Look, I'm sorry about last night."

"It wasn't all bad," she said, then took a sip of the juice.

He looked at her skeptically. "Yes, it was."

For him, it would have been beyond awful to talk to her. She got that. And it had been wrenching to see him in so much pain. But the thing was, they *had* been able to talk about it, and that gave her hope for the future. Now she just needed him to understand how important that process was for them going forward.

"I appreciate that you opened up to me. I'm sure it was hard, but you did it."

He blew out a breath. "That's part of what I'm apologizing for. I shouldn't have dumped all that crap on you. It wasn't fair. It's mine to deal with, not yours."

She reached out and took his hand, and he let her. "We're in this together, Nick. We can share things that are important."

Deep grooves appeared in his forehead. "Okay, sure. Why don't we do something together today? Get to know each other."

She'd already made plans with friends, but she suddenly realized that she wasn't single anymore, and that had broader ramifications than she'd expected. Another person had a stake in simple things like her plans for the weekend. As someone who'd always fiercely protected her independence, it felt a little strange.

"I was going to meet up with some friends for lunch today, but if you think we need—"

"You should go," he said and sat on the end of the bed.

"I'm sorry. I made the plans a couple of weeks ago—back when I was single—and, to be honest, with everything going on, I just forgot to mention it."

"Harper, I want you to go. Our marriage was meant to give you extra support, not get in the way of existing supports."

"Okay, I will." Some time with other people would probably be good to give her some perspective. "What will you do?"

"I need to go for a run. In fact," he said and stood, "I might go now."

"Okay, I'll see you tonight."

He gave her a smile and headed out her bedroom door. It wasn't the same as watching him leave last night—he was going for a run because she already had plans without him—but there was still something vaguely unsettling about watching him go. Perhaps because they didn't have the core bond to their marriage that most newlyweds had, where they knew they could depend on the other.

She looked back down at her tray and picked up the purple flower he'd added. Nick Tate was a good man. Maybe she needed to relax and let things happen naturally. They'd known going in that this wouldn't be easy, so now she just had to trust the process.

Seven

A few hours later, Harper arrived at the Texas Cattleman's Club for lunch with her friend Sophie Prescott and two of Sophie's friends, Natalie Valentine and Emily Knox.

Sophie was already at a table, looking elegant as usual in a mint-green summer dress, her long red hair pinned up in a topknot. Harper had met her about six months ago at a charity fund-raiser, and she'd clicked with her from the start. But ever since Sophie had found love with her boss Clay Everett recently, there was even more sparkle in her eyes, and Harper couldn't have been more thrilled for her friend.

Natalie sat across from Sophie, and they were chatting about something that was making them smile. Harper had only met Natalie a few times, but she liked her, and she really admired the way she was building up her wedding dress design business while still running the Cimarron Rose B&B.

"Harper," Sophie said as she neared the table, and stood to envelop her in a hug. "So good to see you!"

Harper hugged her back, then leaned in to kiss Natalie's cheek. "So good to see you both, too."

Natalie flicked her hair over her shoulders. "I've been looking forward to this. I've been so busy, it's going to be great to unwind with my girls."

"Absolutely, I was—" Sophie said, then froze. "Harper, is there a ring on your finger?"

Harper looked at the gleaming gold band and bit down on a smile. She'd been wondering how to bring the topic up, but it looked like she didn't have to. "Yes, actually, there is."

"As in a *wedding ring*," Sophie said, her expression incredulous. "That has appeared since I saw you just over a week ago…?"

Even though she tried to hold it back, Harper felt her grin sneak out. "There's a story."

Sophie laughed. "I'll just bet there is. Maybe we should wait until Emily arrives so you don't have to repeat it."

Natalie pointed to the main door. "There's Emily now."

"Thank God," Sophie said. "I'm not sure how long I could have waited to find out what happened."

While Emily made her way over, her tall, athletic body graceful as she moved past the other tables, Harper tried to find a way to explain the last week to these women. So much had happened, and she'd stepped way outside her comfort zone. Would they tell her she was crazy? That she'd gone too far? Perhaps a reality check was just what she needed. Especially from Sophie, who was expecting a baby with the love of her life, and so would have a good perspective on the situation. Her opinion was the one Harper wanted the most.

Sophie stood again and hugged Emily. Then, after the greetings were done, she said, "You're just in time, Emily. Harper was about to explain how come she's married now when she wasn't seeing anyone when we last spoke. A. Week. Ago."

Emily's eyes widened. "Oh, that is juicy. Glad I made it in time."

Harper still wasn't sure how much to tell, or how to explain, so she just started talking and figured she'd work it out as she went along. "Do you all know my boss, Malcolm Tate?"

Natalie gasped. "You married Malcolm Tate? He's divine."

"Not Malcolm," Harper said. "He has an identical twin brother. Nick."

"How have I never heard that he had a twin?" Natalie asked. "You'd think I'd remember a detail like that."

"Actually," Emily said, "I think I do remember something about him. Didn't he join the military?"

Sophie nodded as she picked up her glass of iced tea. "Oh, that's right. He married Andrea Miller's sister Melissa. I never could warm to her."

"Have you been dating Nick long?" Emily asked.

Dating? Harper tucked her hair behind her ears. Dating wasn't something she and Nick had indulged in at all.

"We met at Simone Parker's masked ball." She didn't mention that she'd thought he was Malcolm that night…

"That was a great party," Natalie said. "Still, that's fairly quick to a wedding."

Sophie sighed happily. "It must be true love if you knew so quickly. But why didn't you mention you were seeing him?"

"Well," Harper began, looking around at the women's faces. Her gut said she could trust these women with the truth, but it wasn't only her life that would be affected if she was wrong. When Nick's custody case for Ellie was heard, if something leaked out that their marriage wasn't real and his ex-wife's lawyers used that against him, Nick and Ellie would be the losers. So she settled on a half-truth. "It was a bit of a whirlwind, and it sped up when I realized I was pregnant."

Sophie squealed. "You're pregnant, too? How fabulous!"

The others joined in the congratulations and asked questions about how far along she was and details of the pregnancy.

"There's more," Harper said.

"How much more can there be?" Natalie said with an expectant grin.

"I'm carrying twins."

"Oh, my Lord," Sophie said, putting a hand over her chest. "This is the best story I've heard in ages."

The relief and gratitude at her friend's simple acceptance was overwhelming, and Harper had to blink away the moisture seeping into her eyes. Now she regretted that she hadn't shared the news with Sophie as it happened. "I'm sorry I didn't let you know. It just all happened so fast that I haven't had a chance to stop and think."

"Are you happy?" Sophie asked, her gaze serious.

Harper smiled. "I am." It was partly true. When she wasn't worried about the details of how they'd make it work, or the fallout if they failed, she was filled with happiness about the babies. And getting to spend time with Nick was just a bonus.

"Then, that's all that matters. Truly. Hang on," Sophie said and waved a waiter over. "We need something to celebrate with. A bottle of your best nonalcoholic champagne, please."

The waiter nodded, headed for the bar and quickly returned with a bottle and four sparkling glasses.

Once they were filled, Sophie lifted her glass into the air, and the other three women raised theirs to match. "To Harper," she said. "And to Nick, and their marriage. And to their babies. I can't wait to meet them!"

The other two women said, "To Harper," and Harper had to pretend to sip because she knew she wouldn't be able to drink anything with the ball of emotion lodged in her throat.

"Thank you," she said. "That means a lot."

"Actually," Emily said, her eyes dancing as she ran her fingers over the condensation on the side of her glass, "since we're celebrating, I have something, too."

"Really?" Sophie said and sucked in a breath, waiting.

Emily leaned in, practically vibrating with excitement. "I'm pregnant."

"Oh, Emily," Sophie said and jumped up to hug her friend. "I'm so happy for you and Tom."

Harper remembered Sophie telling her about Tom and Emily's tragedy when they lost their child—it had almost destroyed their marriage. They'd only recently found their way back to each other, so the news they were expecting again was like a blessing from heaven, and Harper couldn't have been happier for her.

Emily dabbed at the corner of her eye with her napkin. "Thank you. We're very lucky, and we know it."

"Do you know any details yet?" Natalie asked.

"We know it's a little boy," Emily said, laying a hand over her stomach, "and we've already decided to call him Jeremy Ryan Knox."

Sophie lifted her glass again, and the others immediately followed. "To Emily and Tom, and to little Jeremy Ryan Knox."

"Hear, hear," Harper and Natalie said, and they all clinked glasses.

"Well, y'all know that Clay and I are expecting, so that's three of us." Sophie turned to Natalie. "So now it's your turn. Can we toast a pregnancy for you, too? Make it four for four?"

Natalie coughed out a laugh. "Not a chance of that, I'm afraid. Colby and Lexie are keeping my hands far too full to contemplate another baby. Though there *is* something, and I'm really excited about it."

"Okay, spill," Emily said, still visibly glowing from her own news.

"Brandee Lawless asked me to design her wedding gown and the bridesmaids' dresses. I've had a sneak peek at some of the details of Brandee and Shane's wedding plans, and it's going to be amazing. I'm so thrilled to be a part of it."

"That's fabulous news," Sophie said, raising her glass for the third time. "To Natalie's amazing designs!"

The others joined in, and then they fell into discussing the details of all three announcements over their lunch and another bottle of nonalcoholic champagne.

As Harper finished her last bite of salad, she pushed her plate aside and sat back to listen to these amazing women talk. She'd never had a wide social circle, and making new friends hadn't felt like a priority since she'd moved to Royal a couple of years ago, but she could see that might have been an oversight. And now when the structure of her life was changing in so many ways—would be a good time to address that, so she made herself a promise to stay in touch.

Once their plates were cleared, Emily said, "Has anyone heard anything about Maverick? He doesn't seem to have attacked anyone lately."

"That's a good point," Natalie said. "He was really active for months and months, but I haven't heard anything since he targeted Clay."

Harper ran her hand through her hair, wishing she could be optimistic. But harassment campaigns like this were never that simple. "I don't know anything about Maverick, but, working as a lawyer back home, I saw a couple of similar cases and how things shaped up once the perpetrator was caught. Sometimes the pattern of the attacks is uneven because of factors outside the blackmailer's control. Or they're building up for a bigger attack. I hope I'm wrong, but I don't think we should let our guard down just yet."

Sophie scowled. "Someone needs to stop that man."

Only last month, the anonymous blackmailer who had been targeting residents of Royal had planted a series of fake news stories online about Everest, Clay's business. Even before Sophie and Clay had been an item, Sophie had worked at Everest as Clay's secretary, so she'd taken Maverick's actions personally. And a few months before that he'd sent Emily some photos to make her believe her estranged husband had another secret family. Luckily they'd worked their way through it and were stronger than ever, but there was no love lost for Maverick at their table. Or anywhere in Royal, for that matter.

"I was talking to Sheriff Battle yesterday, and he said there are some good people working on discovering Maverick's identity," Emily said. "As soon as they know who he is, they can arrest him."

Sophie blew out a tightly controlled breath. "Either way, let's hope he's out of our lives before he can hurt anyone else."

"I'll drink to that," Emily said and took another sip from her glass.

Natalie pushed her chair back and put her handbag on her lap. "Hey, sorry to eat and run, but I have to get going."

"No problem," Sophie said. "You have so much on your plate right now."

They all said their goodbyes, and once the three remaining women had settled back in their seats, Sophie reached over and laid a hand on Harper's arm. "Honey, I'm so pleased about all your news. But—how do I say this?"

Harper gave her a reassuring smile. She'd been expecting an extra question or two after the news settled in. "Just say it. I won't be offended."

"For a newlywed who's carrying her husband's babies, you look a little…subdued. Is everything okay?"

Sophie's eyes were kind, and Harper knew her heart was in the right place. Should she confide in her? She didn't have anyone outside the situation to talk it through with—even her mother had been concerned on the phone about whether she'd made the right choice, so she hadn't wanted to worry her more. Perhaps telling Sophie—heck, even saying it out loud—would help her sort through her thoughts.

Since you never knew who was listening at the clubhouse, she lowered her voice. "I'm a little worried about Nick."

Sophie leaned in, her voice a little above a whisper. "He didn't want to get married?"

"It was his idea. He's totally committed to the marriage." She took a sip of her drink, and the other two women waited. "He developed PTSD after his time in the military, and while he's wrestling with that, he's involved in a custody case over his little girl, Ellie, and now to have two new babies on the way and a new marriage... I just wonder if it's all too much." She thought of the look on his face when he'd woken from the nightmare and realized she was there. "And I have no idea how to help him."

Emily opened her mouth as if to speak, then shut it again, her brows drawing together, and then she sucked in a breath as she leaned forward. "I hope you won't mind me butting in since I don't know you that well and I know nothing about PTSD, but I do know something about emotional pain and how it affects a marriage."

Emily hesitated, waiting for encouragement, so Harper said, "You're not butting in at all. I'd appreciate your thoughts."

"After our little boy died, grief tore my marriage to Tom apart. And we let it. If I could have that time over, I'd do something to not let sleeping dogs lie. As I said, I don't know much about your situation, but I'm now a big advocate for trying something. Anything."

The hairs on the back of Harper's neck stood up. *Try something.* The idea was so simple, and so complex, and so right. It was as if she'd turned the headlights on at night—she could see a little of the way.

And a little was enough for now. All she had to do was figure out what to try first, and she was good at that—research, weighing options and making decisions. She could do this. Help Nick.

"Thank you," Harper said, gripping Emily's hand in hers. "I think that's exactly what I needed to hear."

"And in the meantime," Sophie said brightly, "we should order another bottle of bubbles. Between the three of us, we have four babies on the way!"

Harper laughed. "You're right. We'll be Royal's own baby boom."

"To us!" Emily said.

When Harper's car pulled into his driveway after work on Monday, Nick was ready. Living as something of a hermit, he'd fallen into a few bad habits, and he realized now that he had a wife, he'd have to raise his game. After an afternoon session in his home gym, he'd usually shower, throw on the first pair of shorts his hand fell on and then order some takeout.

Today, though, he'd found an ironed pair of cargoes and a T-shirt and even managed to use a comb on his hair instead of simply running his fingers through it. And to really ensure he was turning over a new leaf, he'd made a start on chopping vegetables for a stir-fry.

All in all, he was feeling pretty pleased with himself. Perhaps he could pull off this husband thing.

Well, except for the nightmares and not being able to share a bed. And the constant, all-pervading fear that he was going to let Harper down the way he'd let down Ellie and the men who'd died under his command. And the blackness that surrounded him more often than not, and the constant fight not to let it seep into his relationship with Harper…

Gut churning and hands trembling, he swore and dropped the paring knife onto the board.

When he felt the blackness descending, all he could think was that he'd done the wrong thing by dragging Harper into his world. He should have let her go back to Connecticut, where she'd have her mother and be unsullied by his issues. The idea had been haunting him badly today, which was why he'd made a special effort to be the model husband when she arrived home.

The internal door that led from the garage opened and Harper appeared, her hair swinging around her shoulders as she turned to close the door behind her. He took in her long legs in her knee-length charcoal skirt and how her eyes softened when she saw him, and his heart surged. He knew he couldn't give her up. There was a radiance about her, soul-deep, and he couldn't look away. Now that she was his wife, he'd work as hard as he could, do whatever it took, to keep her in his life.

"Welcome home," he said as he reached for her briefcase.

As she handed the case over, she smiled. "If this is marriage, I think I could get used to it."

"It gets better—I've made a start on dinner," he said, depositing her bag on the coffee table and heading back to the kitchen. "Can I get you a drink?"

"Actually, there's something I want to do, but I'm not sure how you're going to react."

He shrugged and dug his hands in his pockets. "We're still getting to know each other's routines, so it's probably best at this stage that we're up front."

"Okay, but this isn't about routines." With a rare display of nervous energy, she picked up an apple from a bowl on the counter and rolled it from hand to hand, then dropped it back in the bowl. "In fact, it's pretty random."

Surprises weren't something he normally liked, but he was already enjoying this one—or more precisely, he was enjoying watching Harper deliver it. He rocked back on his heels. "Now you have me intrigued. Tell me."

"I heard about this dog today," she said in a rush. "His name is Frank, and he's in a pretty desperate situation." She took Nick's hand and laced their fingers together. "I think we need to rescue him."

His brows shot up of their own accord. A dog? That had been the last thing he'd expected his wife to say. And despite the childhood dogs she'd mentioned to Ellie, she'd struck him more as a cat person. He, on the other hand, was a dog person through and through, and if a dog was in trouble, he was ready to help.

"What sort of rescue?" he said, thinking through the logistics. "Will we need bolt cutters and grappling hooks?"

She chuckled. "You know, you can take the man

out of the SEALs, but… It's nothing that drastic. Can we do it?"

"Tell me a bit more about the dog and its situation."

She started for the steps and said over her shoulder, "How about I tell you in the car?"

Ah, there was his Harper. She might not be a dog person, but she was a good negotiator. In fact, she seemed to have just undercut the negotiations.

He planted his feet shoulder-width apart and crossed his arms over his chest, waiting. She wasn't the only one with negotiating experience.

After a few beats, she retraced her steps and stopped in front of him. "Nick?"

He dropped his hands and grinned. "Sure, let's go take a look."

She leaned into him and threw her arms around his neck. "Thank you."

Unable to resist with her pressed against him, he hugged her tight, just for a few moments, before dragging himself back. The feel of her curves against him was dangerous. It had the power to make him forget they'd agreed to no lovemaking, at least until his nightmares were under control.

As he tried to catch his breath—and his train of thought—he said, "You need to get changed first?"

She glanced down at her silk blouse and knee-length skirt, so he added, "I'm not sure where we're heading, but if a dog needs to be rescued you'll probably want to wear clothes that you can get dirty."

Her forehead creased for a millisecond then cleared. "Good point."

She disappeared down the hall, and he took the couple of minutes before she reappeared in a T-shirt and loose pants to put the vegetables back in the fridge. "Ready," she said.

He looked at the way the pants fell, accentuating her long lines and curves, and was sorry they were leaving the house. But this appeared important to her, so he shook it off, grabbed his wallet and keys, and they set off.

Once they were in the car, he backed out and swung the wheel around to head down the street. "Where am I driving?"

"The Royal Safe Haven Animal Shelter."

An animal shelter? He'd been thinking he might need to do the rescue part and take the dog to a shelter. If they were *starting* at a shelter…

"Harper," he asked mildly, "are we adopting a dog?"

"I don't know." She tapped her fingers on her thighs. "Maybe?"

"We're headed for a shelter. What other option is there?"

"We could foster him until we find him a home. Or maybe we could sponsor him. Or we'll find some other way to save him. It's just that I heard about Frank today and knew we had to do something."

Frank. Good, solid name for a dog. "What did you hear?"

"I don't know much, so it might be better to wait until the shelter manager explains his story." Her voice was confident, upbeat and probably would have convinced a jury.

"Hang on," he said, flicking his wrist over to check his watch without losing his grip on the wheel. "Is the shelter even open now?"

"The manager said she'd still be out back doing paperwork, so she'd let us see Frank."

He had a feeling that more was going on here than she was saying, but he had no idea what. He could press Harper and try to work it out, or he could stop worrying and simply roll with the punches. He chose the latter approach.

When they arrived at the shelter, Harper called a number, and a woman with bright red hair, green eyes and a sprinkle of freckles across her nose came out and unlocked the front door. She wore a friendly smile and a shirt with Royal Safe Haven across the pocket. "Are you Harper?"

"Yes," Harper said brightly. "And you must be Megan. Thanks for letting us in after closing time."

"No problem," the woman said as she closed the door behind them again. "I have a soft spot for Frank."

Harper glanced up at Nick, as if judging his reaction, then turned back to Megan. "Can we see him?"

"Sure. Follow me." The shelter manager led the way past an office to a small room that had a couple of chairs and a dog bed on the floor. Over by the wall, a skinny chocolate Labrador lay with his head on his paws. "This is our meet-and-greet room. I thought I'd bring Frank down here in case you turned up."

"You thought we wouldn't come?" Harper asked.

"Let's say that Frank hasn't been too popular." She turned to the dog. "Have you, sweetheart?"

At hearing his name, the dog moved his eyes to check without lifting his head. He clearly had little interest in what was going on around him, which seemed unusual for a Labrador, especially one who had new people to meet.

Nick crouched down, held out a hand and said, "Hey, Frank. How are you doing?"

Frank glanced over suspiciously, then went right on ignoring them. Something was very wrong.

"What's his story?" Nick asked, still focused on the dog.

Megan leaned back against the painted brick wall. "His owner was in the military and left Frank with family while he was on deployment. Unfortunately, he never came home from his tour, so Frank ended up here."

Nick felt it like a punch to the gut. He could barely draw breath. Since he'd returned home, he'd been tormented by thinking about the people in his unit who hadn't gotten to go home themselves, and here was a dog who was suffering for the exact same reason.

Harper crouched beside him, but said to Megan, "Is he sick?"

"Nope, he's depressed. He's been like this since he arrived. The staff has tried all sorts of strategies to get him to engage, but no dice. We even have trouble getting him to eat. It's like he's given up hope."

Trying not to look big and menacing, Nick got down on his stomach and wriggled over to the dog. He held out his hand, and Frank lifted his head, sniffed in the hand's general direction and dropped his head to his front legs again. Every protective instinct Nick had reared up.

"What's the plan for Frank?" he asked, speaking softly so as not to spook the dog now that he was closer.

"Best-case scenario," Megan said, "he's adopted by someone who understands his situation and emotional state, and they're patient and loving while he recovers."

"Worst-case scenario?" he asked, not taking his eyes off Frank.

"He stays here longer and gives up a little more each day."

Nick held back a shudder. That wasn't going to happen. "Other options?"

"We find him a foster home, so he's out of the shelter while he heals, then he gets adopted."

He looked over at this sad dog who'd lost his human due to the same war that haunted Nick. Frank clearly couldn't stay in the shelter, and what he needed wasn't a temporary foster home. This dog needed someone to commit to him. Someone who'd stay and have his back. Someone who'd never let him down.

Nick drew in a deep breath. He might not have been able to save every man in his unit, but he could save Frank.

He glanced over at Harper, one questioning eyebrow raised, and Harper nodded.

Nick threw Megan a look over his shoulder. "What paperwork do I have to fill out to adopt this dog?"

Harper leaned to look in the backseat of Nick's car at the sad dog who hadn't yet realized his fortunes had turned. All in all, she was pretty pleased with her night's work.

Nick started the engine and said, "We don't have any of the things at home Frank will need."

"Hang on." She picked up her cell to check online for the nearest pet supplies store. "There's a place not too far away that's still open." She gave him the directions, and he turned the car.

When they reached the store, she stayed in the car with Frank while Nick ducked in to grab what they needed.

"So, Frank," she said once they were alone, "you'll like Nick. We're both pretty lucky he picked us."

Though luck might have had a bit of a nudge in Frank's case. Since Emily had urged her at their lunch yesterday to "do something," Harper's mind had been whirring. She'd researched and found two pieces of interesting information. First, programs that matched former military personnel suffering from PTSD with trained service dogs who could intervene and head off some of the symptoms were seeing some amazing outcomes. Getting Nick a trained service dog would have been the ideal solution, but there was a waiting list. She'd made a mental note to do something about fund-raising for the group that was training the dogs to help them help more veterans.

In the meantime, she'd found another piece of useful information—one recommendation for PTSD sufferers was to do something to help someone else. Nick was so concerned about letting someone down again, she wasn't sure he was ready to do that yet. But then she'd wondered, what if the someone who needed help wasn't a person...?

One call to the Royal Safe Haven Animal Shelter and she'd found the perfect dog. The fact that Frank had lost as much to war as Nick had meant they were perfect for each other. Megan had said Frank would need someone dedicated to help him get through his depression, and the look on Nick's face when he'd asked for the paperwork to adopt the dog had told her all she needed to know about that.

Helping Frank would help Nick. And, hopefully, they might even be able to get Frank some training to help Nick even more after that. Win-win.

Nick emerged with his arms full and loaded the bags in the trunk. When he slid into the driver's seat again, she said, "All for Frank?"

"Just a few things to get us started—food, a bed, collar and leash, treats and toys."

"Just to get us started?" His arms had been so full that Harper would have needed two trips to bring all the purchases out.

He arched an eyebrow. "Didn't you tell Ellie you had dogs before?"

"A Great Dane and a Labrador."

"Marshall and Darcy."

He'd listened to her and remembered the names of

her childhood dogs. The thought warmed her heart. "That's right. But I don't remember having so much paraphernalia for them. Maybe things were simpler back then."

He grinned at her. "Or maybe your parents handled that side of dog ownership."

"True." She smiled back. "So have you had a dog?"

"Most of my life." He threw Frank a quick greeting before starting the car again. "Dogs make life better."

She waited while he pulled out into traffic, thinking his words through. There was a gaping hole. "Why didn't you have one already, then?"

He shrugged like it was no big deal. "I was coming and going on deployment, and Melissa said she wasn't interested in looking after a dog while I was gone."

"But you've been divorced for almost two years, and, more to the point, you're not in the military anymore." She turned in her seat a little to see his profile better. "You're not coming and going."

"I hadn't thought about it," he said as he smoothly changed lanes to overtake a slower car.

She didn't believe that for a second. Even if he hadn't considered it, which was unlikely given his reaction to Frank and his comment about dogs making life better, the conversation in the diner with Ellie would have prompted thoughts about a pet dog. There was something else.

"Truth?" she said softly.

He blew out a long breath and rolled his shoulders back. "I guess I didn't think I was in a fit state to take on any big responsibilities."

"But you have," she said, laying a hand over her stomach. "You've taken responsibility for these babies. You didn't have to—you had several chances to bow out. But you stepped up."

He was quiet for a few minutes, until they stopped at a red light. Then he turned to her, brows drawn together. "Before that day Malcolm called and told me you were pregnant, I was basically a hermit." His voice was like gravel, his gaze serious. "The babies and our situation have forced me out of hiding. Prodded me back into the world."

"Are you glad?" she asked, thinking about the discussion she'd had with Sophie and Emily the day before. "Not about the babies, I mean, but are you glad that you've been pushed back into the world?"

He speared the fingers of one hand through his hair. "I think so, but truthfully, I don't know." The light changed to green. His attention returned to the road, and he eased down on the accelerator. "All I know for sure is that I'm pleased you and the babies are in my life, and you three are all tied up in the package of me being out in the world."

She slid her hand over and let it rest on his thigh, offering wordless support.

He seemed to give himself an internal shake, then when he spoke again, his voice was brighter. "Hey, you know who's going to be the most excited about Frank?"

"Ellie," she said, unable to stop the smile as she imagined the little girl's face. "She'll be thrilled."

He laid a hand over Harper's on his thigh. "Seriously, though," he said, and his Adam's apple bobbed down, then up. "I am glad."

She knew he was talking about her and the babies again, and her heart clenched tight. She turned her hand over so they were palm to palm. "Me too," she whispered.

Less than an hour later they were home, Nick's stir-fry was sizzling on the stove and Frank had settled on his new bed, his belly full. He'd sniffed around the yard a little, peed on a plant, then explored a few rooms in the house before curling up in his bed with a sigh. He obviously didn't have high expectations of this place, but then, he wouldn't think of it as his own home yet—he was probably still waiting on his original owner to come back for him.

But he was keeping his gaze on Nick in the kitchen. It could have been because of the food, but Harper was hopeful it was more than that. That they were bonding already.

She wandered over to the stove. "This smells great. Anything I can do to help?"

"Not really," Nick said. "I'm not sure what sort of food you like, so I just grabbed some things from the grocery store today."

She looked into the sizzling pan. "This is exactly my kind of food. But you're right. We should go shopping together when we get a chance so we can see what we both like."

He considered her for a moment, his expression serious. "We've been trying to cover big-picture stuff, but I guess there's still a lot of day-to-day stuff to learn about each other."

She laid a hand over her stomach and glanced from Frank to Nick. "I think we're doing pretty well. We just need to keep moving forward and not let the big stuff overwhelm us."

He smiled at her. "You know what? I think you're right."

Eight

It had been ten days since Nick had married Harper and she'd moved into his place, and a week since he'd adopted Frank, and already he couldn't imagine his life without them. He spent his days with Frank—there was a deluxe dog bed in the downstairs office for Frank's naps while Nick worked on Tate Armor business, then when they needed to work out the kinks, they'd go for a walk together. He hoped to build that up to a run as Frank's fitness increased.

The evenings were for Harper. They'd been taking turns cooking, then sometimes they'd watch a movie. Other times they'd talk about the smaller details of their lives—getting to know each other. But they'd avoided ice cream, and they'd especially avoided all unnecessary touching.

And that part was slowly driving him insane.

Each day he wanted her more. Each hour. Each minute.

He wanted her with a ferocity that surprised even him. And it wasn't just about making love—he wanted the casual intimacy that lovers had. Stealing a kiss when they crossed paths in the hall. Gathering her close when she arrived home from work. Simply touching her, being near her. He wanted it all.

So that night when they stood on his back lawn in the moonlight waiting for Frank to have his final toilet stop before bed, Nick decided he needed to broach the subject.

"I've been thinking about something," he said, gaze on Frank. "You know that if we'd just met tonight, I'd want to date you."

She shrugged. "But we didn't just meet. Our situation is far too complex already."

He turned to face her and dug his hands in his pockets. "What if we kept it simple? And agreed that whatever happens, we wouldn't let it affect our parenting of the babies."

She turned to face him as well, the moonlight catching on her dark hair, making it shine. "What exactly are you suggesting?"

"That we start dating," he said simply.

She arched an eyebrow. "You want to date your wife?"

"More than you can imagine." So much that he'd been having difficulty concentrating on anything else but her.

"I don't know, Nick." Harper folded her arms tightly under her breasts. "There's so much risk, especially for the babies and Ellie."

"But there's also so much potential to have more," he said. "More for us, the babies and Ellie."

For one hopeful moment, her eyes sparkled, then she winced and shook her head. "I think our window of opportunity is gone. Maybe if I hadn't gotten pregnant and we'd met again in a supermarket or socially…"

Her voice trailed off, and she wandered farther into the yard, pausing to rest her hand on top of a dense shrub. Part of him wanted to leave the topic there, but the bigger part of him couldn't let it go, so he followed.

"It's crazy that the one woman I want to date is off-limits because we're already married."

"We had good reasons for putting that intimacy rule into place," she said, her voice sounding strained.

That was true, but there was something undeniable between them. Something that wasn't fading away by ignoring it. "My last tour taught me is that life is short and unpredictable. And I don't want to live with regrets."

"But that's my thinking, too." She ran her fingers through her hair, pulling it tightly back from her face as she spoke. "I don't want to move our relationship into new territory and come to regret that."

"Harper, we're never going to be a couple who only react to each other like friends." He reached for her hand and laced their fingers together, relishing the sizzle as her skin slid along his. "We have chemistry. If we continue like we are, the tension will eventually explode. The best way forward is to manage that tension as much as we can."

There was silence for three beats, four.

"Okay, if—and I'm only saying if—we tried to manage this, how would you see it working?"

"We'd date. We'd treat it as a totally separate thing from our marriage. The marriage is the legal agreement that we entered for the sake of the babies, and Ellie, and Tate Armor, and to ensure you had support." He took an infinitesimal step closer. "Dating would be just for us."

Frank came ambling over, finished with his nightly business. Nick gave him a short pat, and, obviously realizing the humans might take a while, Frank lay down at their feet.

"*How* would we date, though?" Harper asked. "We've just watched a movie together on the sofa. Our life together has moved past dating scenarios."

"Just because we live in the same house doesn't mean we can't go out on dates. Maybe we fool around if the mood strikes, the way a dating couple would."

Her brows drew together. "Sex is a line in the sand for me in this relationship."

"It doesn't have to be sex." He took another small step closer. "Holding hands. Making out. Just like if we were any other dating couple. And we see how it goes. If it's making things messier, we haul it back again."

She pulled her bottom lip into her mouth as she

considered and he watched, mesmerized. He'd kissed that plump lip. What he wouldn't give to be able to kiss it again right now. To pull it into his mouth and gently bite down...

She released her lip and blew out a breath. "If we keep crossing that line and then retreating, the line is going to get completely blurred."

"It comes down to one question." He took her other hand as well and brought them together—all four of their hands in one grip. "Harper, do you want to do this?"

She closed her eyes tight, as if in pain, before opening them and meeting his gaze head-on. "Of course I *want* to. That was never in question."

"Then let's give it a try. We're both well aware of the potential pitfalls, which means we'll be on our guard for them. Let's just give it a try."

She opened her mouth to say something, hesitated, swallowed hard, then nodded. "Sure. Okay. But it needs to be a trial, just to see how it goes."

He wanted to haul her against him and hold her, but he knew the only way forward was cautiously, so instead he just said, "Deal."

But inside he was smiling.

The next day, Harper was unwrapping a sandwich at her desk so she could work through her lunch break when she thought she heard Nick's voice float through her open door. She glanced through the plate-glass walls of her office to the open-plan area outside. Sure enough, Nick was wending his way through the desks, heading for her. Her heart stuttered to a stop at the sight of him, and when it kicked back in, it beat faster than before. Oh, the way that man moved—prowled—was a sight to behold, and the movement of each step pulled his clothes against his body, hinting at a physique toned by his daily workouts. She only just managed to restrain a sigh of appreciation.

A few people greeted him as Malcolm, and, not bothering to correct them, he said a casual "Hey" and kept moving.

She shook her head. The idea of mixing the two men up was ludicrous. They might look the same, but Malcolm was a warm, sunny day to Nick's dark, brooding night. Of course if she hadn't recognized that he wasn't Malcolm on the night of the masked ball, she couldn't expect that people who were only seeing him pass by to realize it. Besides, Nick was the silent partner—there were probably a few people working here who didn't even realize Malcolm had a twin who owned half the company. Still…

He reached the desk just outside her office, and her assistant, Tom, glanced up to check if she was available then waved through the man he obviously thought was Malcolm. Nick barely seemed to notice that he was being given permission—his gaze was firmly locked on her. A delicious shiver of anticipation raced down her spine at the sparking intensity in his eyes.

Tom must have noticed something was a little off—perhaps since Nick hadn't slowed to greet him the way Malcolm normally would have—so he turned and watched as Nick entered her office.

He gave her a lopsided grin and said, "Hey."

"Hey, yourself." She stood and rounded her desk. "This is a surprise."

"Since we started dating, I thought I'd drop by and take you to lunch. You know. On a date."

"I was expecting we'd do things at night or on the weekends." And, to be honest, she hadn't expected anything quite so soon.

He took her hand and linked their fingers. "It wouldn't have been much of a surprise that way."

She coughed out a laugh. "I guess not."

Over his shoulder, she noticed there was something of a scene unfolding on the other side of the plate-glass walls. Several people had dropped by Tom's desk—some had taken the time to grab some paperwork so they could at least pretend they had a legitimate reason to be watching the events unfold, but others weren't bothering with trying to be subtle. Of course, office life at Tate Armor was normally fairly routine and boring, so an event like the man they thought was the CEO walking into the company attorney's office and holding her hand would be an interesting diversion, and word spread fast.

Normally she was a private person and would cringe at being the center of a scene. But with Nick smiling at her, she couldn't bring herself to care. Instead, she looked back to him and murmured, "We have an audience."

She looked down at their linked fingers and wanted

to just focus on this new feeling of being courted by her husband, but she couldn't completely ignore her coworkers, so finally she glanced up at Nick again.

"I haven't told anyone here yet."

He tucked a strand of hair behind her ear. "About the babies, about the wedding or about me?"

"Any of it," she admitted, trying not to wince but probably failing. A couple of times she'd almost told Tom but had changed her mind each time. She'd never shared much personal information before, so she hadn't known how to start.

Nick raised an eyebrow. "No one noticed the wedding band?"

She shrugged. "I don't tend to hang out at the water cooler."

"I seem to have let part of your secret out," he said, clearly pleased with himself.

"It seems you have."

With a finger under her chin, he tipped her face up to look into her eyes. "Are you sorry?"

"Not really," she said, and realized it was true. "I wasn't deliberately keeping it a secret, I just haven't told anyone. I'm normally fairly self-contained."

He smiled knowingly. "Seems I'm not the only one with hermit tendencies."

"I suppose that's true." She'd never thought of herself as a hermit or considered cutting herself off from people the way Nick had since he'd returned home, but she had always been a bit of a loner. "You've been physically isolating yourself, and it's probably fair to say I emotionally isolate myself."

"Well, maybe you *used to* emotionally isolate yourself," he said. "Now you're married with two babies on the way and stepmother to a three-year-old."

"And I'm adjusting," she said, attempting a reassuring smile before adding, "slowly."

"How about we help it along a little?" His voice was deep and smooth and laced with mischief, daring her to put a foot out of line.

"How?" she asked, equal parts curious and wary.

Raising an eyebrow and keeping her gaze, he lifted her left hand up to shoulder height and pointed to her wedding ring, then his own. The murmurings floating through her door increased to a buzz.

She laughed and rested her forehead against his chest. "Not into subtlety?"

"Not really my forte." He stepped back, smiled generously at the crowd then placed a hand on Harper's stomach. The assembled group—which, by now, was almost the entire staff of the company—gave up any pretense of being there for any other reason but gawking. They clearly thought they were at the unveiling of a secret office romance between the CEO and the company attorney—the most delicious piece of gossip all year. Most people were grinning, a couple had their mouths open in a wide O, and Tom gave her a double thumbs-up.

Harper blew out a breath and caved in—she gave her coworkers a little wave and then put her hand over Nick's on her stomach.

"You know," she said, "it's going to be impossible to get any work done for the rest of the day."

"Worse things have happened."

"You should care about this, as a co-owner of the company."

"As a co-owner of the company, I find this scenario more amusing and satisfying than a few extra hours of completed work."

The elevator pinged, and the doors slid open, revealing Malcolm. The murmuring stopped as the actual CEO walked through, glancing around, clearly wondering why the people he paid to work at these desks weren't actually doing that.

Then he caught sight of his brother, and understanding dawned on his face. He headed over to them. The silence dissolved, and the gathered people realized that they hadn't just witnessed a scene between Harper and Malcolm—which was juicy enough—but this was, in fact, a rare sighting of the fabled identical twin. The buzz began again, people not even bothering to whisper anymore as they shared tidbits of information they had about the other partner in Tate Armor.

"So," Malcolm said as he reached Harper's office door, "the newlyweds can stop traffic. That's as good an omen as any for a marriage. Though I'd be careful with these displays of unprofessional behavior in the office, Nick. One of the company owners is ex-military, and I hear he takes the professionalism of his staff very seriously."

Nick rested an arm around Harper's shoulders. "Our marriage doesn't need good omens—it's doing fine on its own. In fact, I'm here to take my wife out to lunch."

Malcolm checked his watch, his face deadpan. "Is it that time already? I haven't had lunch, either. I might join you."

Harper was enjoying the banter between the brothers, but Nick clearly wasn't in the mood. "This is a private lunch date," he said and tugged on Harper's hand.

She grabbed her bag and let him lead her to the elevator. Nick hit the down button, the doors whooshed open and they stepped in. As she turned, she saw all her coworkers and boss gathered together, having been thoroughly entertained by her and Nick, and instead of finding it intrusive or a nuisance, as she would have a few weeks ago, she felt stirrings of mischievousness. Like she was playing hooky by going out to lunch...and enjoying it. Just before the doors closed, she bit down on a grin and gave another little wave to the crowd.

When they reached the security desk just inside the building's front doors, Nick stopped to thank Steve, the guard, and pick up Frank, who'd been sleeping behind the desk.

The dog even looked a little pleased to see him. When Nick had left him there on his way to get Harper, Frank had seemed to accept it as if he was being handed to yet another owner. The fact that he seemed to be moderately pleased to be back with Nick was an improvement.

Harper gave Frank a hello pat and waved to Steve. Once they were outside, she said, "I've never seen any of the guards here provide dog-sitting before."

"We knew each other in high school. Besides, he's a navy vet, and when I told him Frank's story, he offered to help out with him if we needed it."

He didn't need help for Frank, but he'd been thinking about organizing some fund-raising for a charity he'd read about that looked after the dogs of military personnel while they were on deployment. Maybe he'd come back another day and see if Steve was interested in getting involved as well.

"So," Harper said when they reached his car, "I'm guessing with Frank tagging along, we're not going to a fancy restaurant?"

He opened the back door, and Frank jumped in, turned a couple of times and lay down.

"If it's okay with you—" Nick closed Frank's door and turned to Harper "—I had the kitchen at the TCC clubhouse put together a gourmet picnic basket."

Her eyes lit up. "That sounds perfect."

Feeling pretty happy that he'd planned something for their first date that put that look in her eyes, he held her door as she slid into her seat, then rounded the car and settled in on the driver's side. Before he started the ignition, he reached for her hand again.

"I want to show you a special place. We might not make it back in the hour that Malcolm allots for lunch, but we shouldn't be too late."

"As you pointed out," she said, grinning, "I have

quite a bit of vacation saved up, so a little late will be fine."

Nick drove them to a spot just outside town that not many people knew about. It was pretty much still in its natural state, with a small waterfall—nothing too spectacular, but the rhythmic sound of the water was one of the few things that helped center him. And he wanted to share that with her.

He parked, let Frank out and grabbed the picnic basket and a blanket from the trunk while Harper took in the setting.

"This place is amazing," she said, resting her hands on her hips, watching the waterfall. "I've never been here. How did you know about it?"

His lungs cramped tight. He'd known the question was coming—anyone would have asked in this situation—yet it still managed to blindside him. He carefully took a breath, then another. Harper turned curious eyes to him.

He cleared his throat and gave half an answer. "I've been coming here for years. Sometimes there are other people, especially on weekends, but often it's deserted."

"Well, I love it." She smiled, seemingly satisfied with only half an answer, and his lungs released their tension, allowing him to draw in blissful gulps of fresh air.

Frank trotted over, sniffed around a little and relieved himself on a tree trunk, then came back to where Nick was setting up the blanket and curled up on a corner. Watching the simple, practical movements of his dog helped Nick regain his equilibrium.

Harper slipped off her heels, knelt on the blanket and helped unpack the basket. She held up a small container of mixed olives. "This all looks fabulous. Did you choose the food?"

"I left that to the clubhouse kitchen." He reached in and came out with a sealed plastic bag that contained a silver bowl, a small bottle of spring water, some dog treats and a ball. He chuckled. He'd asked for a picnic basket, and when they'd asked how many were going, he'd said just him and his wife. He'd added, "And my dog," as an afterthought, simply because he liked saying he had a dog, not thinking they'd include anything for Frank. It was nice of them. He appreciated attention to detail in customer service—he'd have to send them another tip later.

He poured the water into the silver bowl and offered it to Frank, along with one of the treats. The Labrador sniffed the treat then carefully took it from him and chewed. It tore at his heart that Frank still felt the need to be so careful about everything.

Gaze on his dog, Nick casually said, "I've been wondering something."

As Harper pulled the last contents from the basket—china plates and thick, luxurious napkins—and laid them out, she threw him a look over her shoulder. "It just so happens that plying me with delicious food is a good way to get me to answer just about anything."

He grinned. "I'll file that away for future reference."

She settled back on the blanket, stretched her long legs out in front of her and leaned back, resting her weight on her hands. "What do you want to know?"

"The other day you said you'd heard about a dog and we had to rescue him."

"Mmm-hmm," she said, her tone noncommittal.

He reached over and rubbed Frank's soft ears. "How, exactly, did you hear about him?"

"Ah." She busied herself serving food onto their plates. He wasn't sure if it was a strategy to avoid eye contact or not, so he waited until she sat back and met his gaze. "Well, to be honest—"

"Always the best policy," he interjected, amused.

"—I called the Royal Safe Haven Animal Shelter and asked Megan to tell me about their special needs dogs. She ran through a few, then when she mentioned Frank's history, I asked her to hold him for us."

"Right." He'd started to suspect as much. Something in her story had always been a little suspicious. "So, why make the call to the shelter in the first place?"

"Because the wait was too long for a trained service dog."

He opened his mouth to reply, then shut it again. She'd lost him in that last leap of logic. "You know, this might be easier if you just start from the beginning."

She handed him a plate piled high with food, then took hers and put it down on the blanket. But she didn't start eating. She stared at her food for long moments, then lifted her gaze to him. Totally open—no avoidance, no games.

"I wanted to do something to help you with what you're going through. So I did some research into PTSD."

He stilled. The last thing he wanted was Harper thinking he was a charity case or pitying him. "Learn anything interesting?" he asked, trying for a casual tone and unsure if he'd achieved it.

She nodded, clearly warming to her subject. "I saw some really good outcomes for veterans with a trained service dog. The dogs could head off anxiety attacks and wake their person from a nightmare."

He'd heard similar things. "A friend mentioned once that he knew a couple of guys who had them."

"But there was a waiting list, so I kept researching." Her eyes were shining with enthusiasm, so he bit into a roll and lost himself in her light as she talked. "Another piece of advice I found was to do something for someone else. To help someone. But I knew you were worried about letting someone down again, and you already felt your plate was full with me, Ellie and the babies, so that wasn't a great plan. It could make things worse rather than better."

He winced. That was a harsh but fair assessment. Still, he didn't want her feeling like she was a burden to him. "Harper, I don't think of you as—"

But she interrupted him. "It's okay, Nick. I know what you mean. And anyway, then I had an idea— what if the someone you helped wasn't a person?

What if it was a dog who needed you as much as you needed them?"

Her plan finally made sense. "So you called Megan and asked about special needs dogs."

"And you met Frank and fell for him at first sight. Now that I think about it," she said, her mischievous smile peeking out again, "you seem to have a habit of committing to people and dogs before getting to know them."

"Since it worked so well with you, I thought it was worth a shot with Frank." He glanced at the dog, who carried the weight of hope and expectation on his furry shoulders. It was a lot for a boy dealing with his own issues. "Harper, what if he doesn't help me?"

Her gaze didn't falter. "Then we'll have a gorgeous family pet for Ellie, the babies and us."

"Sounds like a perfect plan," he said.

She popped a juicy olive in her mouth and chewed, watching him carefully, and when she'd swallowed, asked, "Are you mad at me?"

She'd lied by omission and had been poking around, researching something he found intensely personal. He should be annoyed. Strangely, he wasn't.

"I'm grateful. That you researched it and came up with a strategy, and for Frank himself." Frank looked up at his name, probably hoping for some cheese, and Nick ruffled the top of his head. "I think he's already helping."

She'd been right—it had been good to have someone else who needed him during the day when Harper was at work and Ellie was with her mother. He'd even taken to talking to him on their daily walk. Frank was a good listener.

They sat in companionable silence as they ate their picnic lunch and listened to the waterfall. When they were done, Harper lay back on the blanket, her hands behind her head, and Nick stretched out beside her, feeling surprisingly content.

"So now I'm wondering something," she said, looking up at the clouds.

"It just so happens that delicious food and good company make me feel like sharing, too."

"This place." She waved an arm around to encompass their surroundings. "Tell me how you found it."

Ah. He shouldn't have been surprised she'd circled back around to the topic. After all, she was a lawyer. He braced himself and exposed a guarded part of his heart. "My dad brought me here. He said it was our place."

She rolled to her side, her cheek resting on a palm. "Not Malcolm, too?"

"Our parents were always careful to let us do things together when we wanted, but to let us have our own experiences, too."

"That's a good tip for a mother-to-be of twins," she said. "Why did he choose this spot for you and not Malcolm?"

Good question. In some ways it was such an obvious thing, but how to explain it?

"Malcolm was always more...social than me. He and our mother are two of a kind. Dad and I, on the other hand—" he glanced around at this place that had always been theirs "—well, we always craved a bit of space. Quiet space."

She was silent for long moments, and when she spoke, her voice was gentle. "How long ago did he pass away?"

"Nine years." Though it didn't feel that long at all—occasionally Nick even forgot he was gone. "It was his heart. He'd had problems before, and he was on a transplant waiting list, but it gave out before they found one."

"Oh, Nick." She scooted closer and leaned into him. "I'm so sorry."

He wrapped an arm around her shoulders and allowed himself the luxury of absorbing the nearness of her and her unquestioning support when he needed it. "In some ways we were lucky. He knew there was a chance he wouldn't make it, so he had time to say his goodbyes. Not everyone gets that."

There had been lots of family chatting, teasing and laughing—just as his father had wanted. And there had also been time for his father to have deep, one-on-one talks with each of them.

One time when they'd been alone, Nick's dad had gripped his hand and told him—not for the first time—that he was the strong one, and he'd have to look after his mother and Malcolm. It had made a deep impression on his soul, and he'd done his best ever since. When things were hard, he often thought of his father's face as he'd said those words and it was enough to keep him going, keep him moving forward.

One thing he was glad about was that his father

had seen him in uniform before he died. Swiping away tears, his father had told him how proud he was, and it had been one of the best days of Nick's entire life. He'd tried to be the man his father had expected him to be, which was one of the reasons he'd found struggling with his PTSD so hard. A strong man—the man his father had wanted him to be—would have handled it, right?

He glanced over at Harper—an intelligent, brave woman, who had barely blinked when he'd told her about his PTSD, and had even gone out of her way to research strategies to help. Just the thought of what she'd done for him made his chest ache in a way it never had before. An ache just for her. He reached for her hand, gripping it tight, and, as she smiled at him, a sliver of optimism shone through the dark parts of his mind. If she didn't think he was a lost cause, then maybe, just maybe, there was hope for him still.

Nine

It was just past midnight, and Nick was sitting out by the pool, watching the moon, Frank snoring by his feet.

He hadn't been able to sleep, so earlier he'd sat up in bed with Frank across his lap and begun, hesitantly, to tell his dog some of the less painful stories from his time in the military. It had been strange at first, but he'd read some articles online about talking through upsetting memories with a dog. As Frank had lain attentively, with no judgment in his gaze, it had slowly become easier. He'd talked for maybe an hour, and his shoulders felt a fraction lighter at the end. Sleep had still evaded him, though, so he'd come out here to watch the shimmering water in the pool and breathe the cool air. Frank—with his job done—had decided to catch a nap.

Movement at the sliding glass doors caught his eye, and he turned to find Harper in a long nightdress coming over to him. Bathed in the pale blue moonlight, she seemed ethereal, and the gentle night breeze draped the fabric against her body, revealing the growing roundness of her belly. The sheer perfection of her stole his breath. She was a goddess—so much more than he would ever deserve.

"Did I wake you?" he asked when she reached him. Uncertain if she was a light sleeper or not, he'd tried to be quiet when he'd been near her room.

She shook her head and grimaced. "Leg cramps. I was hoping walking might ease them."

He was instantly more alert. Cramps were no laughing matter—experience from both training and missions had taught him that. "Has the walking helped?"

"Not so much." She rocked from her heels to her toes and back again.

He cast an assessing glance over her. "Is it just your legs?"

"Well," she said, drawing out the word as if not really wanting to admit more, "my back is aching."

He pushed to his feet. In some respects he might have been a poor choice as a husband, but this was one thing he could do something about.

He slipped an arm around her waist. "Come on, I have a couple of ideas."

As they started walking, she leaned in to him and whispered, "Thank you."

"I haven't done anything yet."

"You have," she said and looked up at him, her sweet brown eyes filled with emotion. "You're here and you're willing to help. You have my back. They're things I really appreciate."

"You're welcome," he said around a lump in his throat. To have a woman as strong as Harper Lake say that to him…it meant a lot.

They reached her bedroom door, and he released her. "You go curl up in bed. I'll be back in a minute."

Once in the kitchen, he quickly made up a hot water bottle. When he returned, he found her already in the bed. He tucked the hot water bottle against her back, then sat on the side of the bed, feet on the floor. "Here, give me the leg that's worst."

She lifted her right leg to lie across his lap, and he went to work, gently at first, looking for any knots and tightness, then easing it with rhythmic hand movements.

"The pregnancy books said I might get cramps, so I shouldn't be surprised." She offered a half smile that made him wish he could scoop her up, hold her tight and protect her against anything that might hurt her.

Instead, he kept massaging her leg and said, "What else do the books say we should be looking out for?"

"So many things," she said, watching his hand sliding along her calves. "Those books are quite scary, to be honest."

He'd been home between tours when Ellie was a baby, but he'd been away for a big chunk of Melissa's pregnancy. He was only realizing now what he'd missed and was determined not to let any details pass by this time. "Okay, so we'll ignore the books for the moment. Tell me what it's like for you."

As he rubbed the muscle, up and down, gently digging his knuckles in, she opened up about the little things she hadn't shared before now. At one time he might have thought he was tough as nails, that war had hardened him, but listening to Harper describe the miracle of pregnancy, the ways her body was changing as it grew his babies, he could practically feel his heart melt into a puddle.

They changed positions so he could do her other leg, and he asked more questions, drawing out her own feelings of wonder about the experience.

"You can probably stop now," she said with a soft smile.

Her eyes were drooping, so he ran his hands one last time over her calf, as much for himself as for her, then pulled the sheet up over her shoulders.

"Sleep well," he said and reverently kissed her forehead. Reluctantly, he steeled himself to walk away and leave her until morning.

"Nick?"

He didn't dare look back at her, knowing his willpower was already stretched thin. "Yeah?"

"Stay with me." She lifted the sheet as invitation. "Just for tonight, stay and hold me."

His stomach rolled and sank. He'd been the one to propose marriage, and he'd been the one to suggest their new dating arrangement. No question, he'd been the one pushing their relationship forward. And now Harper was finally asking for something, wanting more…and it was something he couldn't give.

"Harper, I'd do it if I could, but you know I can't."

She sucked her bottom lip into her mouth and bit down, her gaze watchful, uncertain. "Is this just about your nightmares?"

She thought that he didn't want to be in her bed? That he didn't dream of waking wrapped around her warm body? "I promise, nothing else could keep me away from you."

"I don't care about them." She wriggled up to a sitting position against the headboard.

God, the temptation of the idea. *Of her.*

"Sleep is essential when you're pregnant." He said it like it was a mantra.

"It's just for tonight." She glanced at her bedside clock. "Or what's left of it. I'll sleep better if you hold me."

In asking for this, he knew she was going out on a limb. She'd been so cautious about taking their relationship too far or too fast up until now. And *this* was the thing she chose to ask of him. The one thing he couldn't grant her.

His chest ached from having to deny her, but he had no choice. "Harper, I can't. You know I can't."

He'd have given anything in that moment to climb into that bed and lie with her all night. If he ever healed from this damn illness and was able to spend his nights wrapped around her, he'd never take it for granted. Not even once.

"Harper, I'm so damn sorry."

"It's okay," she said, but there was hurt in her eyes. Hurt he'd put there with what was, in effect, another little abandonment, and that pierced something deep in his chest. He squeezed his eyes against its power, brushed a kiss over her forehead and walked away before he could change his mind.

Nick sat on the end of Harper's bed, looking at the paint swatches she'd taped to her wall. They'd spent the evening measuring the nursery for furniture, and thinking about colors and decor.

"I'm not sure I can look at another yellow swatch. I might have reached my limit of yellow."

"Not a problem," she said, her voice holding a note of teasing. "This one isn't yellow. It's lemon sorbet."

He groaned, then chuckled and fell backward to lie across the width of her bed. "Just come and sit for a few minutes and give me a break."

"Would you rather look at the seven swatches of various whites for the trims?" she said, but she came over anyway and lay down beside him.

As he stared up at the ceiling, he felt her hand sneak into his, and he squeezed it tight. And though he never would have predicted it a few months ago, there was nowhere he'd rather be than lying side by side with this woman, talking about setting up the nursery and holding hands. It was scary how much he simply wanted to be near her.

"How do you think us dating is working out?" he asked mildly.

Two days ago he'd thought he might have blown

it by not staying the night when she'd invited him. Thankfully, she'd been fine the next morning, acting as if nothing had happened, and he'd been beyond relieved. They'd gone out to a movie and dinner last night and talked the whole way home about the movie's plot, so he hoped they were back on solid ground again. But Harper was sometimes hard to read, and he knew he had to check in with her.

"I think we're doing fine," she said.

He rolled his head to the side so he could see her. "You seriously mean that?"

"So much." She leaned in to him and brushed her lips over his. His eyes drifted closed to savor the feeling. Harper had been so adamant about not adding intimacy into their arrangement that he wouldn't push. But then her lips brushed past his again, and he kissed her back.

He still couldn't believe he'd come so close to not having this woman in his life. If he'd gone in to the Tate Armor office at any time in the past two years that Harper had worked there, he would have met her. Instead, they'd met at a masked ball where he hadn't known who she was and she'd thought he was his twin brother.

That very first time he'd laid eyes on her, every thought in his mind had fled. All he could see, all he could register, was her. She'd worn a gold mask that she held in front of her face by a long stick that served as a handle. She'd lowered it for maybe a minute while she ate a canapé. No one else was watching, but Nick was. She wasn't just beautiful; there had been something else that called to him. Something he couldn't name but that was soul-deep and unable to be denied.

And she'd been watching him. The realization at the time had damn near stalled his heart.

"Do you remember when we met?" he asked, running a lazy hand up and down her arm.

She snuggled closer into him. "I'll never forget that moment."

He wanted to believe it but refused to let fantasy get tangled up with their real story—not when their real story was already enough—so he had to call her on it. "You thought I was Malcolm."

"My mind thought you were Malcolm. But the rest of me thought you were…"

"Yes?" he whispered in her ear, then sucked the lobe into his mouth.

"Mine," she said on a sigh.

She reached up to cup the side of his face, the motion making her top ride up. His fingers found the exposed stretch of skin along her side, across her stomach.

His eyes drifted closed again. He was lost in the feel of her under his hands now and the memory of her then. "You were wearing a glittering gold mask at first."

"And you had a black mask that covered half your face," she said, her breath coming a little faster and her hands slipping under his shirt.

He had a brief thought about their agreement not to bring lovemaking into their marriage, but surely they were past that by now? And Harper didn't seem to be slowing down. They'd agreed that their dating would be a trial, so he decided to give in and let what had been building between them play out this once.

Needing more, always needing more, he pulled her top higher, then, as she raised her arms, lifted it over her head before quickly dispensing with his own shirt. He settled back, satisfied his hands now had a wider range of skin to explore.

"I love it when you do that," she said, turning over to face him, then kissing him lightly, her lips brushing over his, teasing, luring.

"I aim to please," he murmured. He stretched out on the bed and adjusted her so she was lying along his body, gravity ensuring their skin-to-skin contact was firm, just the way he liked it. "You wore a dress the color of autumn leaves."

She arched an eyebrow. "A dress you had off me in less than an hour from first sight."

"Which was no disrespect to the dress," he said as he unhooked her bra and threw it over the edge of the bed. "I dreamed about that dress every night until I found you again."

And that would have been a whole lot sooner if she hadn't run before he could get her number. The day he'd discovered she was pregnant and they'd reconnected, she'd admitted that she'd freaked out that first night, thinking she'd just slept with her boss. It was understandable, but still a shame that they'd lost those months.

A smile slowly spread across her face, even as she

pushed his trousers and boxers down his legs. "You dreamed about me?"

"Oh, yeah." They had been most excellent dreams—almost enough to make him not hate falling asleep at night. He stroked his hands down her bare back, still marveling that he didn't need those dreams anymore. She was here with him. Touching him with as much urgency as he touched her. "And you weren't just in my dreams," he continued. "Thoughts of you filled most of my waking moments as well." He unsnapped the clip at the back of her skirt and tugged it, then her underpants, away, leaving all her glorious skin available to his roaming hands.

"Tell me," she said as she kissed a trail along his collarbone.

When her tongue flicked out and joined her lips on their mission, he had to pause and find his breath before he could reply. "When I was jogging, I could hear the sounds you made." She lightly bit his shoulder, and his breath became jagged.

"Tell me more," she said, moving down his chest.

"Whenever I closed my eyes, I could see your eyes, and the way they burned with wanting." He speared his fingers through her hair as she kissed his abdomen. "When I stood under the shower spray, I could feel the smoothness of your skin."

"Keep going," she said, but then her teeth grazed across his abdomen and he stopped being able to talk at all.

Deciding to even things up a little, he rolled so she lay beneath him. She gasped, and he grinned. Surprising Harper was one of his favorite things to do. Then, supporting himself on one arm, he snaked a hand down to the juncture of her thighs, moving in rhythm until she whimpered—another of his favorite things to do.

"Now you tell me," he practically growled. "Did you think about me?"

Finding his gaze, she nodded. The emotion in her warm brown eyes melted something inside him, and he slowed his hand.

"I was confused," she said, "because I'd see Malcolm at work and not feel anything, but when I was home, in those moments between sleeping and waking, where my mind wasn't in control…it was you." He saw her throat work as she swallowed. "Everything was you."

Beyond words now, he leaned in and kissed her, less gently this time, and she matched him move for move. Her skin was awash with heat, almost singeing his fingers, and he couldn't get enough. He was addicted to her.

"Hold that thought," he said, reluctantly summoning the willpower to tear himself away, and took off at a run for his own room, returning seconds later with a foil packet. Once he lay back beside her, she took the condom from him and sheathed him with efficient movements. His heart kicked into a higher gear.

He entered her in one fluid motion, finding himself home again, unable to stop the groan of pleasure that came from deep within him. She whispered his name, then again, and it was like a vow, a promise, and he whispered her name back, sealing the vow between them. As he moved inside her, he gave himself over to her. Surrendered himself. To Harper. She enveloped him, besieged him, possessed him.

She gripped his shoulders, and the bite of her nails in his flesh made everything more real. It was too much, not enough, too much, then her release took him further, wanting, reaching, then imploding into electric light, floating, happy. With her.

Snuggled together on the bed minutes—or hours— later, she stirred, and he found the energy to rearrange their bodies so she was tucked into his side.

"Nick," she whispered against his skin. Then she lifted herself onto an elbow and met his gaze. "Stay with me tonight."

"Don't ask me that," he said, his voice gruff.

"Please?" she added softly.

His heart tore in two. Denying her two nights ago had been hard. After what they'd just shared, denying her was close to impossible.

The memory of the horror on her face when she'd witnessed his nightmare still haunted him, and it rose again now, chilling the blood in his veins. What kind of monster would subject anyone, let alone the woman pregnant with his babies, to that kind of torture? He leaned away and prayed for strength. Spending the night in her bed was out of the question. He wouldn't let her go through that experience again.

The problem was, if he couldn't stay, and he couldn't walk away—what other option was there?

"Please, Nick," she whispered and laid her hand flat over his heart. "Stay with me tonight."

Maybe it was because it wasn't the first time she'd asked, or maybe it was the way she'd said "please," like all she wanted in the world was him, but he couldn't hold out against her another second. He nodded, and twenty minutes later when they were finally ready for bed, he grabbed the edge of the sheet and slid down beside her, his legs rubbing against hers as he got comfortable.

She sighed as he wrapped an arm around her waist and snuggled her back into his chest a little more. Carefully, he dropped a kiss in the place where her neck sloped into her shoulder, the scent of her warm skin filling his head, wrapping around him, luring him into never letting her go.

But she was pregnant and needed solid sleep, and she wouldn't get that if he slept, too.

Only one of them could sleep. And no way in hell would he let her be the one to miss out.

Her breathing changed into a soft, steady rhythm, and despite his own sleepiness, he called on all his SEAL training, every ounce of self-discipline he had, and refused to give in to the pull of slumber.

And, as the dark of night eventually gave way to the early morning light, he realized something: holding her all night while she slept might be difficult, but it was also a blessing. He was damn lucky to have an angel like Harper in his life, no matter the complications, and he'd never let himself forget that.

Harper checked on the tray of cupcakes in the oven and began a batch of pink icing. Nick would be back soon with Ellie for their day together, and she wanted freshly baked treats to greet her. This time she'd be ready, unlike when they'd first met two weeks ago. Sure, it was practically bribery to make the little girl like her, but Harper didn't mind—if a judge asked Ellie if she liked spending time at her father's house, she wanted Ellie to have no hesitation.

Since Nick had started sharing Harper's bed at night, they'd become closer. And their lovemaking had only gotten better, too—her hormones were going crazy, and carrying twins, she had double the amount swimming through her bloodstream.

Even Frank seemed to be improving with Nick's love. He was more interested in food and had begun to relax when they gave him affection. He still hadn't made the step of approaching them for attention, but he was making progress, and that's what counted.

The sound of the garage door opening floated through the house just as she pulled the cupcakes from the oven, and a few minutes later Nick emerged from the internal stairs with Ellie on his hip, one hand over her eyes.

He threw Harper a smile before saying to his daughter, "Are you ready for your surprise?"

"Yes!" she yelled, pumping her little arms in the air.

Staying a safe distance from Frank, who was lying on his soft bed, but still keeping the dog in his line of vision, Nick took his hands away from Ellie's face. She blinked, looked around, then her gaze landed on Frank. She stilled, not moving a muscle, then burst into tears and threw her arms around Nick's neck, holding him in a death grip with her face buried in the crook of his shoulder.

Alarmed, Harper moved closer. Was Ellie scared of real life dogs? Should she do something?

"Do you want me to take Frank outside?" she whispered.

Nick looked up from soothing his daughter, but his face was smiling. "Come closer," he said. Harper did, and he added, "Listen."

Ellie was sobbing, but on each exhale were the words, "Thank you, Daddy, thank you."

"She's happy?" Harper asked, confused.

He kissed his daughter's forehead and held her a little tighter. "This is a very happy girl. Just a bit overwhelmed." He smoothed back Ellie's hair and crooned soft words to her.

Harper's eyes misted over—partly in reaction to Ellie's joy and partly from watching a father's love in action. She couldn't take her eyes off her husband—the scene was too beautiful.

It was a good five minutes before Ellie had calmed enough to actually meet the dog. Nick explained to her that Frank had been sad, so she had to be quiet and gentle with him, and Ellie took that advice to heart, practically becoming Frank's nursemaid. Nick supervised, and Harper retreated to the kitchen to ice the cupcakes and watch the father-daughter bonding time.

The morning was going even better than she'd hoped. Fingers crossed, the rest of her plan for the day would be as much of a hit.

After a while, Nick brought Ellie into the kitchen. "Do you like Frank?" he asked.

Her face was earnest. "I love him, Daddy."

"Do you want to know whose idea it was to bring Frank into the family?"

Ellie nodded her head solemnly.

"Harper's." Ellie turned wide eyes on Harper, and Nick continued. "She called the Royal Safe Haven Animal Shelter and asked about all the dogs, and when she heard about Frank, she thought he'd be perfect for us. So she came home to get me and we went to meet him. We both loved him right away, so we brought him home."

Ellie grabbed Harper's hand. "Thank you, Harper. Frank is the best dog in the *world*."

Emotion thickened her throat, and she had to swallow hard before she could reply. "I'm glad you like him."

Then Ellie's eyes landed on the iced pink cupcakes on the counter and widened more. "Who are they for?"

"They're for all of us," Harper said. "I was thinking we might want to have a tea party today. What do you say?"

"Yes! Can Frank have one, too?"

"Dogs shouldn't eat pink cupcakes, but we have some other treats here that Frank will like even better."

"I will give it to him," Ellie said as if that settled the matter, and Harper smiled at Nick.

"Absolutely, you can," Nick said.

Once they were set for their tea party—all sitting cross-legged on a picnic blanket on the living room floor, Frank sprawled between Nick and Ellie, a cupcake on each plate —Harper brought out a bag she'd left on the coffee table.

"We bought you something," she said as she handed the bag to Ellie.

Ellie drew in a quick breath. "A present?"

More of a way of explaining the news to her through a picture book, but it probably counted as a present, too, so she nodded and said, "Yes, it is."

The little girl pulled the book from the bag, ran a hand over the shiny cover and passed it to Nick. "Can you read it to me?"

"Sure." He held out his arms, and Ellie scrambled into his lap. As she snuggled into his embrace, Nick began to read the story of a little girl who gets a baby brother. Ellie watched the illustrations on each page, enthralled. When he finished, Nick said, "We have some news for you."

Ellie looked up expectantly into her father's face. "Am I getting a baby brother?"

Nick chuckled. "Actually, you're getting *two* baby brothers or sisters. We just don't know if they're boys or girls yet."

"Really and truly?" Ellie asked, seeming close to tears again.

"Really and truly," Nick said solemnly.

She threw her arms around his neck. "Thank you, Daddy!"

Harper sighed happily as she watched them. Ellie

was having a pretty good day, between the babies, Frank and the pink cupcakes, and there was something so very satisfying about being part of the team that made a little girl so happy.

When Ellie released her father, she looked over at Harper and said, "Can I keep it?"

"Of course you can, honey, it's yours." Harper settled back against the sofa and laced her fingers over her stomach. Maybe she was starting to get the hang of this stepparenting thing.

Ellie picked up the book from Nick's lap and put it on her own outstretched legs, stroking her hands over the shiny cover. "I love new books."

"I do, too," Nick said. "Harper bought me a new book, too."

Still playing with the cover, she turned curious eyes to him. "What's yours about?"

"It's about a policeman who looks for clues," Nick said.

Ellie nodded as if that was just the right plot for one of her daddy's books. "Does the policeman get a new baby at the end, too?"

"No, at the end of mine, the policeman solves the case then gets a new job."

Harper's breath caught. *He knew the ending?* She'd bought both books yesterday, and Nick had only started his when they went to bed last night. The book wasn't short. If he'd finished the entire thing, he must not have slept a wink...

Nausea that had nothing to do with the pregnancy rolled through her stomach. He'd agreed to sleep with her at night, but it appeared no actual sleeping was happening for him. She thought back—she was always the first to fall asleep, and he was already awake when she woke in the mornings.

He'd been lying to her.

They were in the middle of a crazy situation, a marriage of convenience to achieve several goals— but at the core, she'd thought at least they could depend on each other. That they were open and honest with each other.

Their marriage might be a practical arrangement, but that only made it worse—you don't go into business with someone you know you can't trust.

"Daddy?" Ellie said as she jumped up. "Can I give Frank my teddy?"

"I'm sure he'd like that, sweetheart. Which one will you give him?"

"Can Harper help me choose?"

Harper glanced over. This overture from Ellie was exactly what she'd been hoping for—Nick's daughter had accepted her enough to want her help with something special. And yet, she couldn't feel the joy the way she'd hoped. Not when she was starting to question everything.

Ignoring the confusion buzzing through her brain, she found a smile for the little girl. All she could do was compartmentalize the thoughts about her marriage, focus on Ellie and talk to Nick once they were alone.

So she helped Ellie choose a teddy for Frank from the collection in the room she had at Nick's house—

"A brown one like him, so he will know it is his"—
and then walked back out to the living room with
the little girl.

Nick had cleared away the plates and assorted clut-
ter from the tea party and was back on the blanket,
sitting beside his dog.

Ellie carefully sat beside Frank and placed the
teddy on his front paws. "This is for you," she said.

Frank sniffed it over, nudged it a little with his
snout, then laid his head on it. Harper suspected he
wanted to lay his head on his paws anyway and the
teddy just happened to be there, but, either way, Ellie
was thrilled.

"He likes it!" she said. "Good boy, Frank."

For the rest of the day, as they played with Ellie
and had a barbecue lunch, Harper felt like she was
simply going through the motions. Nick had said
he'd sleep in her bed, but he'd been staying awake all
night. He'd purposefully hidden what he was doing,
lied about it. It was vital that she understand the reality of Nick's condition, partly because she could be
called on to make a statement to the court in Ellie's
custody hearing. She was a lawyer and would already
be lying to a court of law—that was bad enough. To
be caught in that lie because her partner in crime had
withheld information from her? That would be bad
for all of them.

More importantly, she was bringing two precious
babies into the world with this man—she had to be
certain she knew how he was handling his condition,
and that he'd tell her of any changes, so she could

mitigate any issues for the babies and for Ellie. Sure, she knew he would plan around any sleepovers Ellie might have in the future so she wasn't affected by his nightmares, but Harper would be irresponsible not to wonder if there was anything else he wasn't telling her...

How could their arrangement survive if she couldn't be sure what was truth and what was lie?

Ten

Nick arrived back from dropping Ellie at Melissa's house feeling like crap. It was getting harder and harder to let his daughter go—one day with her every two weeks wasn't nearly enough time. The only thing that made it close to bearable was knowing Harper was waiting at home.

But when he walked into the living room, emotionally wiped out, he found her sitting on the edge of the sofa, strangely alert. And she wasn't happy—there was an air of tension radiating from her.

"Everything okay?" he asked warily as he dropped his keys and wallet on a side table.

"We need to talk." Her voice was clipped and precise.

Nick winced. It was worse than he'd thought. He headed for the sofa and sat across from her, needing the angle to see her expressions—he hadn't seen Harper angry before, so he didn't want to be flying any more blind than he already was.

He paused to take a breath, then plunged head-long into whatever was waiting for him. "Have I done something you're not happy about?"

She crossed her legs, and the foot hanging in the air bobbed to a silent beat. "You could say that."

Hell. He squared his shoulders. "Tell me."

"The question is whether you were going to tell me," she said, her cheeks flushed pink.

Pulse racing now, he scanned through everything that had happened since breakfast. They'd definitely been happy together then—Harper had kissed him as he left and made all sorts of promises about tonight. He'd ducked out to pick up Ellie, introduced her to Frank, and Ellie had thanked Harper for getting the dog. Harper had seemed really affected by the moment, so things were still good then. After that they'd had a picnic on the blanket, told Ellie about the babies, then had a barbecue. In fact, they'd both been with Ellie all day—there hadn't been much chance to do or say anything controversial, so he was at a loss.

"You'll have to give me a hint," he admitted.

She reached behind her to a long table that ran along the back of the sofa that had photos and other paraphernalia on it. She grabbed the murder mystery he'd been reading—and which he'd left beside the bed—and held it up. "When did you read this?"

His stomach dropped as it all clicked into place. "Last night."

"The entire book?" she asked calmly, but her eyes were steady in their focus. "In one night?"

"Yeah," he said and blew out a breath.

She tossed the book onto the cushions beside her. "Have you slept at all since you started sharing my bed?"

He shook his head and admitted the truth. "I normally catch a nap in the morning before I start work. I don't need a lot of sleep."

She crossed her arms under her breasts. "You've been lying to me."

The accusation was like a slap to the face, even though it was true. He *had* been lying to her—lying by omission—and it had felt wrong every time he hadn't told her. But he'd chosen the lesser of two evils, and he still thought it had been the right call for them. Convincing Harper of that would be another matter, though.

"I'm sorry I haven't been honest about when I sleep, but you have to see that it's the best option for us."

"How?" she asked. "Explain that to me."

"Harper," he said gently, "I saw your face when you witnessed me having a nightmare. It's burned into my memory banks—there's no way you can pretend it didn't scare you."

"Yes, it did scare me. Of course it did—I had to try to make sense of your anguish and agitation while I was half-asleep. I had no warning, so it was a shock. Now that I know, I'll be prepared if it happens again."

"You need your sleep while you're pregnant and

working full-time. Being woken each night because of my nightmares is not good." He scrubbed his hands through his hair. "Look, I can see why you're upset— I'm just not the man I used to be. I can't do all the things I used to."

"No," she said, her voice low. "I'm upset about the lie. We're in the middle of this intense situation to-gether—we married to protect your custody of your daughter from your ex-wife and her fiancé. To protect our babies' relationship with both their parents. To protect Tate Armor from Maverick. All while you're dealing with the aftereffects of fighting a war on the other side of the world. Plus we can't tell anyone about our marriage arrangement except Malcolm, just in case Melissa finds out. In the midst of this, all we have is each other."

"You're right," he said. "We do have each other."

"The thing is, we never had a bond of love to hold us together. This was always a partnership between two people who have mutual goals, and any feelings and intimacy that developed were a bonus."

He cocked his head to the side. "We're in agreement about all of this."

"All right, then. Here's my point. What we have is a shared situation, as well as respect and trust. And if you take out the trust, you undermine the agreement that everything else was built on."

It suddenly all clicked into place. "Okay, I get it." Being completely open with the mess that was in his head wasn't second nature to him, and it wasn't an appealing thought, either. But he'd committed to this marriage, and he had a lot to lose, starting with relationships with his three children. He needed to step up his game. "I'll keep you in the loop with what's going on for me. And if I slip up, just ask. I promise I'll do my best to explain."

"Thank you." The word was whispered so softly, he barely heard it. "And I promise not to pressure you to give more than you feel you can. If you want to go back to sleeping in your own room, that's okay with me. And the alternative is okay, too—staying the night with me, risking that you'll have a nightmare and trusting that I'll be able to handle it."

The fear rose up and threatened to overwhelm him, but he wanted to do this. Wanted to try. Could he? Dare he?

He moved over to her sofa and sat beside her. Then he stepped over the edge of the cliff. "If you really mean it, I'm willing to try actually sleeping with you."

She wrapped her arms around his waist and leaned her head on his shoulder. "I really mean it."

He pulled her tighter and hoped like hell that he hadn't just made the biggest mistake of his life.

It was a few hours later, when they'd had dinner and were ready for bed, that Nick found himself in Harper's room, wanting desperately to climb under the covers with her but still not sure if he could risk it.

Causing Harper pain or distress went against everything he believed in, and yet, he'd already agreed to stay the night with her. And actually sleep. Breaking his word also went against everything he believed in…

She stroked a hand over the sheet and smiled at him. "Come on in, the water's fine."

At war with itself, he took a step, then another until he reached her. "Are you sure?"

"Nick," she said, her gaze steady, "you need to trust me. And trust in my capacity to cope."

Still torn, he sat on the edge of the bed. "It's not that I don't trust you."

Her expression changed, and he saw glimmers of the courtroom lawyer. "When you were in the military, you were part of a team. Everyone had a job to do, and you had to trust one another to do your jobs, right?"

"Right," he said, warily.

"This is the same. You need to let me play my part." She pulled his shoulder until he lay down beside her. "Promise you'll trust me and you'll go to sleep?"

He knew, without a shadow of a doubt, that this was a turning point in their relationship—tonight could bring them closer or push them apart.

He let out a long, controlled breath. Whatever the outcome, he'd made the decision earlier when he'd agreed to sleep with her, so it was time to step up to the plate and put his words into action.

He wrapped an arm around her waist. "I promise."

"Thank you," she whispered and snuggled her back into his chest.

He pulled her closer, adjusted the pillow under his head and let his eyes drift shut. After a few minutes of listening to Harper breathe and trying to relax himself to sleep, the world began to fade.

* * *

*A flash of light amid the dirty dark of night...
Ground shaking, walls shaking... Diving for cover...
Screaming from all directions... Another flash...
Noise filling the air leaving no room for anything
else, not even oxygen... Screams of the dying... Trying to shout orders but smoke stealing his voice...
His men. Where were his men? Searching... The
stench of vomit and blood...a pile of clothes—no,
a man. Gregson. Lifeless... No! Oh, God, no... So
sorry... Flames... Shouting... An arm. Moving rub-
ble. Adams. Alive... Dragging to safety, going back
in... Flashes and noise... More dead... Screaming...
Sorry, so sorry...*

A soft voice floated through the darkness, soothing, telling him he was safe. It was a beautiful voice,
one that stirred his soul and drew him away from
the horrors still clinging to him. But the darkness
wouldn't release its grip that easily, and the place between sleep and wakefulness was the worst...

In dreams, there was still a small hope that he'd
find more of his unit alive this time. That he'd save
them. He would have thrown himself between his
team and danger to protect them, no question. But
each time present-day reality intruded, he'd remember all over again that he hadn't saved them. And
there was nothing he could do to fix it now. Adrenaline pumped through his system, urging him to act.
To do something.

The voice was still there, anchoring him. Harper's

voice. And another sound. Soft whining from his other side.

Heart thudding against his ribs, he pried his eyes open to see Harper filling his vision, her achingly beautiful face surrounded by a soft halo of light.

"Hey," she said gently.

He couldn't yet form words, and he didn't know what he'd say anyway, but he did know she was the only person he wanted to see right now. The only one who could make the darkness inside seem a little more bearable. Though, even as his arms wanted to reach for her, he locked his muscles tight to stop them. Dragging her further into his darkness would be selfish.

More than that, he didn't deserve the comfort. The nightmares were a fair penalty—reliving the horrors was the least he deserved. After all, some very fine people hadn't made it through to be *able* to remember it.

This was his penance.

His father had told him to stay strong. Good advice. No matter what was in his memory banks, he should be able to handle it. He drew another shuddering breath and clenched his hands to stop them shaking. He had to be honest with himself—he was clearly *not* handling it. Worse, Harper could see his failure. She was bearing witness to his shame.

Something wriggled on his other side, and he became aware again of the soft whining in the background. He turned to find Frank on the bed, stretched out alongside him, burying his face in Nick's side.

"I didn't invite him," Harper said. "When I woke up and realized you were having a nightmare, Frank was already here, leaning in to you, making those noises."

Nick put an arm around Frank, and his dog settled against him, feeling solid and reassuring. The presence gave more comfort than he would have expected. There were treats in that dog's immediate future. Just as soon as Nick mastered basic things like breathing and moving again.

He began to silently count his breaths, a technique he used to calm his body and slow his pulse, relying on the steady strength of both Harper and Frank to help. Three breaths in, Harper lay down and wrapped her arms around him, holding him. It was more than he deserved. She was always more than he deserved, more than he should accept, but, God help him, he couldn't bring himself to push her away. Pathetic as he was, he wrapped his arms around her and took the comfort she offered, grateful she at least hadn't been horrified this time.

As Harper watched her husband beside her, she was determined not to let the tears pressing at the back of her eyes form. He wouldn't want them. Instead, she lay quietly, letting him deal with whatever was in his mind at his own pace, trying to be a calm presence.

Calm was a big ask when she was torn between despair at seeing him in pain and hope because he hadn't shut her out this time. She rubbed his tense shoulders and settled for calmish.

After long minutes, he pulled himself up, but still he didn't push her away—he sat on the edge of the bed, his elbows resting on his knees, his head hanging low, as if he was still trying to regain his breath. She swung her legs around to sit beside him, laying a hand gently on his back so he knew he wasn't alone.

Without looking at her, he reached out and snagged her other hand, bringing it to rest on his thigh, their fingers tightly entwined. Her heart stopped dead at the meaning in the simple gesture, then roared back to life, flooding her body with emotion. By reaching for her instead of pushing her away, Nick had let her though a major barrier.

"Thank you for trusting me," she whispered. "For sharing the parts of you that I know you'd rather keep hidden."

He didn't look at her, barely moved beyond his chest rising and falling more roughly than it should. "I'm still not feeling great about dragging you into this mess."

He might not feel great about it, but she was happy to be dragged anywhere with him. It was being left behind that hurt.

She stood and drew him to his feet. "Together, we can face this."

"I'm starting to believe we can face anything together."

"I think you're right."

Pulling gently on his hand, she led him into the

attached bathroom, and once they stepped past the door, she lifted onto her toes and kissed him. He returned the kiss—not one of passion, but sweetness, trust, bearing witness to the depth of their relationship. Tears stung at the backs of her eyes, but she didn't realize one had fallen until he wiped it from her cheek with his thumb.

Wordlessly, she stepped back and turned the shower on, testing it with her hand as the water warmed to the perfect temperature. Then, their fingers again entwined, she stepped in, tugging his hand to bring him in after her. One corner of his mouth lifted in a shadow of a smile, and he followed. Her pulse kicked up a notch. She released his hand and placed her palms on his chest, gently pushing him under the spray.

As she soaped him up, she allowed herself the luxury of admiring his body, loving the ridges and hollows, the scars as well as the smooth perfection. And he allowed her—turning when she nudged him, letting her take the lead.

"No need to think," she said. "Just feel."

His shoulders relaxed a fraction more as he gave himself over to her. His body followed her movements as if they were in a dance, his breaths becoming fast and shallow, matching hers.

She wanted to give him this—the mindlessness of his body's reaction, all traces of the images that had haunted him banished under the weight of desire. So she touched him the way she'd learned he liked to be touched, lightly feathering her fingertips over his abdomen, kissing along his collarbone, scraping her nails over his back.

"Harper," he rasped against her throat. Her skin felt too tight for her body, and his hands roaming only made her restless for more.

With a hand under one of her knees, he picked her leg up and brought it around his waist, then gripped her hips and lifted her. She leaned her weight against the cool tiles at her back and wrapped her other leg around him.

As the shower spray fell against her skin, Nick thrust forward, filling her, moving in a rhythm that quickly took her to the brink, then higher, building, higher, past the point she could contain it anymore, until she was bursting, flying free, and even before she could land, she felt him follow her, shouting her name. And in that moment, she felt more connected to him than she had to any other person, and she could believe that nothing would ever tear them apart.

Once she regained her breath, she lowered one leg to find the shower floor again—even slumped against her, he'd still been holding her weight. He released her, placed a tender kiss on her lips, then ducked his head under the water. This time he soaped up his hands and washed her, then when they were done, he dried her off and wrapped her in a thick towel.

"Thank you," he said, his gaze holding hers. She didn't pretend to misunderstand. He wasn't thanking her for what she'd done with her body—it was more than that. He was thanking her for looking after him. For caring. For accepting him.

"We're in this together," she said. "We're a team."

He swallowed hard and nodded before gathering her against him and holding tight.

Eleven

Harper arrived at Natalie Valentine's bridal store at the Courtyard Shops five minutes late for their lunch date with Sophie Prescott.

Natalie met her at the door, her shoulder-length red hair swept up in a messy ponytail, and handed her a glass of champagne.

"Sorry I'm a little late," Harper said as she slipped inside.

"Don't worry." Natalie smiled. "I'm running even more behind than that. The champagne is to make up for it. It's nonalcoholic for you and Sophie."

Harper tasted the cool drink. "Random glasses of champagne make up for just about anything."

"Come on, Sophie's already over here. I'm doing a fitting for Chelsea Hunt's bridesmaid's dress, and she said she doesn't mind if you two are here while I finish up."

Natalie showed her over to a set of sofas where Sophie—her own glass of champagne in hand—was already sitting with a gorgeous woman with glossy honey-brown hair around her shoulders. Harper had never spoken to Chelsea before, but she'd heard nice things from other people, so she was pleased to have the chance to meet her.

"Harper, this is Chelsea. She's Brandee Lawless's maid of honor, and I just need to make a couple of quick alterations to her dress before we can go." She turned to the other woman. "Chelsea, this is Harper Lake. She's an attorney over at Tate Armor."

"Nice to meet you, Harper," Chelsea said, holding out her hand. "Tate Armor. Isn't that Malcolm Tate's company? That man is seriously gorgeous."

Caught off guard, Harper felt heat creep up her neck to her cheeks as she shook the other woman's hand. Though it wasn't Malcolm she was thinking about.

"Oh, I'm sorry," Chelsea said, her gaze roaming over Harper's face. "Did I put my foot in my mouth? Is there something between you and Malcolm?"

"Not Malcolm," Sophie said. "His identical twin brother, Nick. Who one assumes must be just as seriously gorgeous."

Just as seriously gorgeous. Harper almost laughed. How did she explain that the two men were identical, yet looked nothing alike? One was easy on the eyes. The other made her burn with want and fire and need and *love*…

She stilled. As soon as the word formed in her mind, she knew it was true. Hard to believe she'd fallen in love so quickly, but there was no other way to describe the intensity of her feelings for him. The way her heart skipped a beat whenever she saw Nick or heard his voice. Or even thought about him.

The other women were still looking at her, waiting for her to confirm that Nick was as gorgeous as Malcolm. She gave a quick nod and slipped into a seat on the sofa.

Natalie took a step back. "Can you just excuse me a minute? I need to check a couple of things on the dress."

Sophie raised an eyebrow. "We don't get to see it?"

"Not until the wedding, along with everyone else," Natalie said with a smile, then disappeared into another room.

"So, the last time we were together, there was lots of juicy gossip," Sophie said good-naturedly. "I'm hoping for at least as much today."

Chelsea glanced up. "Juicy gossip? You can't say something like that then not explain."

"Well," Sophie said, grinning, "the juiciest of all was that Harper here got married since we'd last seen her less than a couple of weeks before."

Chelsea's eyes widened. "To Nick Tate?"

"Yes," Sophie confided. "And they're expecting twins."

"Okay, that *is* juicy." She turned to Harper. "I'm impressed—you make good gossip."

Chuckling, Harper raised her glass to her, said, "Thanks," and sipped the amber liquid, hoping the conversation would flow in another direction. She was in no state to chat coherently. After all, she'd only just realized she was in love with her husband.

"Now, Chelsea," Sophie said, "your turn. What have you got that will go well with this glass of bubbles?"

"Okay, there is something." She took a mouthful of her champagne, then grinned.

Harper grinned back, feeling a little light-headed. The drink was nonalcoholic, so it had to be from her realization about Nick, but she liked Chelsea already, so she was happy to share her good mood. "Anything you say won't go any further," she said and touched a finger to her lips. "Our lips are sealed."

"Well—" Chelsea glanced around, clearly trying not to smile "—I've been seeing a fair bit of Gabe Walsh since we've been doing the best man–maid of honor duties for the wedding."

"Gabe is another man who's seriously gorgeous," Natalie said, poking her head around the door from the other room.

Chelsea bit down on her lip and seemed to lose herself for a moment before continuing. "We were out at Brandee's Hope Springs Ranch the other day, doing a few things for the wedding, and there was... how about we say there was a little extracurricular activity."

"Did you kiss him?" Sophie asked, her eyebrows raised in happy surprise.

"I will say this," Chelsea said with a dreamy look in her eyes. "That man has a mouth made for kissing."

There were several happy sighs around the group seeing the expression on Chelsea's face, then conversation moved on for a few minutes until Natalie refilled their glasses and said, "So, any news of Maverick? I haven't heard anything lately."

"Still seems to be quiet," Sophie said with a shrug.

Chelsea glanced around. "Actually, I have something to confess on that front."

"You figured out who he is?" Sophie asked, her eyes wide.

Chelsea shook her head. "The next best thing. I called an old friend, Max St. Cloud, to come help with the investigation."

"What could this Max do that the town's not already doing?" Natalie asked as she came out and took a measurement of Chelsea's shoulders before disappearing again.

"I used to do a bit of hacking when I was younger, and so did Max, which is how we met. Honestly, he's a genius." Chelsea's smile held a small flicker of pride in her friend.

"Actually," Harper said, thinking the case through, "he could really help. Since Maverick has been stalking and threatening people through email and on social media and he's obviously stolen files to use as blackmail, an ex-hacker on the team is a great idea."

"Any new tactics are worth a shot," Sophie said. "Maverick has already caused too much damage."

"Hear, hear," Natalie said coming back out to the main room. "And on that note, I'm done. Chelsea, you're free to go."

"Thank, Natalie," Chelsea said, reaching for her bag. "I can't wait to see the finished dress."

Sophie stood. "Chelsea, you're more than welcome to join us for lunch if you'd like."

"That's so sweet of you, but I have a couple of other maid of honor duties to take care of, so I'll take a rain check. See you all later!"

As Chelsea swept through the door, Harper turned to look at her friends and had a moment of blissful satisfaction. Everything in her life was going so well. She had a wider circle of friends than she'd ever had, her pregnancy was progressing nicely, things with Ellie were going great and her marriage with Nick had never been better. In fact, she was in love with him. Which was more than she'd dreamed possible for their fledgling relationship. It was as if the pieces of her life were all falling into their slots, and a sense of bone-deep contentment and happiness settled over her.

The only thing that could make her life even better was to share her feelings with Nick. Now she just needed to find the perfect way to tell him.

Nick stood as his ex-wife joined him at a corner booth in the Royal Diner. Now that things were going so well with Harper and he could see them making a family with the babies, he'd decided it was time to do something about Ellie's custody situation, too. He'd asked Melissa to meet him—just the two parents, on their own, looking out for their kid's best interests. He'd mentioned the idea to Harper for a lawyer's take, and she'd said it made a lot of sense. What surprised him was that Melissa had agreed to it.

Not knowing how to greet her, he stuck his hand out. This was new territory for them. In the past, they'd dated and been newlyweds, expectant parents, spouses in a crumbling marriage, then exes at war. What were they to each other now? Only time would tell.

Melissa looked at his outstretched hand, then reluctantly took it for a few seconds before dropping it.

"Thanks for coming," he said as they took their seats.

She gave him a steely glare that carried a note of warning. "I almost didn't."

He understood that, and she'd never been one to hold back, so her honesty was a good sign. "What changed your mind?"

She shrugged. "First and foremost, I want what's best for Ellie. It's what I've always wanted."

"I appreciate you giving this a shot." A trace of optimism started to stir in his chest. Maybe they could work out some sort of agreement and he'd be able to be a proper father to all three of his children.

A waitress came, and they ordered drinks. When she'd left, Melissa speared him with a glance and said, "Okay, let's cut to the chase. What do you want?"

"More time with Ellie. To be a bigger part of her life."

She dismissed that with a flick of her wrist. "That's what the lawyers are for—to work out those arrangements."

"Come on, Melissa," he said. "We're the two people who care most about her. We're her parents. We should be able to work it out between ourselves."

"And you honestly think that would be best for Ellie, given your…"

"PTSD," he supplied. "I've made some solid progress with that." Thanks mainly to Harper and her limitless patience and support.

Their drinks arrived, and Melissa fiddled with the straw in hers for a few moments before excusing herself to go to the bathroom. Nick sat back in the seat. Getting her here had been step one. Step two was telling her what he wanted. Now all that was left was to get her to agree. When she came back, he'd push more and they'd avoid a legal battle.

As soon as she was out of sight, her fiancé strolled over and stood at the table.

"Guy," Nick said, narrowing his eyes. "I didn't know you were coming."

He gave a smarmy, insincere smile. "Look, Melissa is too nice to say it, but we both know what kind of man you are."

"And what kind is that?" he drawled.

"A screwup."

From someone whose opinion mattered, that might be insulting. From this pathetic excuse of a man? Borderline amusing. "And how do you figure that?"

"You're not quite right in the head anymore, are you, Nick?"

He barely held back a sigh. "I have PTSD, if that's what you mean."

"And that's not all."

"I think it's time you left," he said, trying to keep his tone even despite his growing annoyance.

Guy reached into his jacket pocket and withdrew a handful of tablets and laid them on the table in front of him. Nick recognized them immediately—over-the-counter and prescription pills. All painkillers. For several seconds he couldn't breathe. All he could see was the pills. He hadn't seen that many together since he'd beaten his addiction to painkillers after his last mission. And here they were, inches from his hand, their siren's song calling him.

Then Guy whipped out his phone camera. "I think our friend Maverick could do some real damage with this photo—"

There was movement to his left followed by Melissa's voice. "Guy, I didn't know you were back." Then she noticed the pills. "What the hell, Nick?"

"They're not mine," he said, his voice gravel as he forced his lungs to work. "Guy dumped them here."

"Guy?" she said.

"I'm sorry, baby," her fiancé said, his voice dripping with slime. "We know he's going to relapse at some point and put Ellie at risk. I just thought if we speed it along so it happens before the custody case instead of after, then it would be better for all of us."

"You did this?" Melissa looked appalled. "Guy, this has to stop."

"You know I only want what's best for you and Ellie. And, seriously, Maverick would love something juicy like this. We post it online and he'll find it—he's really good at sniffing a story out."

Nick could hear the argument between his ex and her fiancé going on, but his gaze was stuck on the pills, and he felt his skin breaking out in a fine sheen of sweat.

"This," she said with a sweep of her arm, "is crossing a line. You'd better leave."

Surprised, Nick looked up at that, to see Guy blink and cast a furtive glance around before focusing back on Melissa. "But, baby, I'm doing this for you."

"Someone who crossed the line for one person will cross it again, and I can't have that around Ellie."

Guy frowned. "Hang on, what are you saying?"

"This is the last straw. It's over, Guy." She took off the sparkly ring on her left hand and held it out to him.

"Over *him*?" Guy asked incredulously.

"No, over you," she said, hands on hips. "Because now that I've seen you pull this stunt, I'll never trust you again."

"Baby girl," he said, but she cut him off.

"You can sleep at a hotel tonight and we'll work out the rest tomorrow."

Clearly stunned, Guy simply stared at her, then visibly regrouped. "Okay, sure. We'll talk about this more tomorrow when everyone is calm again."

Guy kissed her on the cheek and sauntered out. Melissa watched him go then turned back to Nick. "I'm sorry. You and I don't see eye to eye on a lot of things, but you didn't deserve that."

He gave a tight nod, looking at her but keeping the pills in his peripheral vision.

"And you know what?" She blew out a breath. "You're probably right that it's time the two of us sat down and did discuss Ellie's arrangements. Let me deal with Guy first and I'll give you a call in a few days. We'll work something out."

"Sure." Nick kept his poker face in place despite knowing his voice was strained. "That would be good."

Melissa turned and headed out the door, which left Nick alone at the table. With the pills. His hands were trembling with the need to take one. Just one. His heart raced. One couldn't hurt, could it? Just one. He swallowed hard.

Logically, he knew it would never be just one. And that was the problem—he knew that and he still wanted one anyway.

He checked, and no one was watching. The angle of the booths meant that it was hard for others to see unless they were standing right in front of him. Very carefully, he slid the pills closer and filled his trouser pockets with them. Then he pushed to his feet, threw some cash on the table to cover the drinks and a tip, and left.

He made it to his car, and all he could think about was which pill he'd have first.

And where he'd go to take it.

What he'd drink to wash it down.

And how many he could manage in one day.

Harper arrived home with her heart overflowing. The realization that she loved Nick had her practically floating all the way to his house. They'd married for the babies—to fall in love as well was more than she'd dreamed possible. A fairy tale come to life.

When she walked inside, she found Nick sitting on a stool at the kitchen counter, his gaze bleak. Her stomach clenched tight.

"What's happened?" As she neared him, she reached out, but he turned away from her, so she stilled. "Nick?"

He opened his mouth to speak, then closed it again. His Adam's apple bobbed in his throat. Unease prickled across her skin. Something was very wrong. She glanced around, and her gaze landed on a thin stack of papers on the kitchen counter. It was too far away to make out the wording, but she'd seen countless legal documents in her career. Enough to recognize this as one.

She took another step and reached for the papers. Nick held up a hand to block her, then dropped it.

"Harper," he said, his voice raw. "This is not—"

But she'd seen the first lines. These were divorce papers. And their names were typed in black print. The room began a slow spin around her.

"You're divorcing me?" she asked, not quite be-

lieving it was possible. Waiting for him to explain
how this was part of a grand plan…

"Yes."

The word was plain and stark, and all the air
rushed from her lungs. *He was leaving her.* Visions
from when she was six years old began to flood her
mind—the devastation as the front door closed behind her father, the tears, the desperate heartache—
but she pushed it aside. This was different.

This was *Nick.*

It made no sense. They'd been so happy. They'd
moved past their biggest hurdle and were now sleeping together through the night. What could possibly
have changed for him? He'd kissed her this morning
when he'd left to meet… *Melissa.*

Could his ex-wife have sabotaged their marriage?

She swallowed against the lump forming in her
throat before she could get her voice to work. "What
did Melissa say to you?"

"She was surprisingly reasonable," he said.
"Things only went bad when Guy showed up."

Everything inside Harper wanted to demand answers, to push hard against the threat to her marriage,
but the small part of her brain that was listening to
rational thought knew that wasn't a good idea. She
called on all her self-control and calmly said, "What
did he say?"

"His usual bluster and crap." To a casual observer,
Nick's face would appear expressionless, but she was
no casual observer. There was a slight tightening
around his jaw; the edge of his lips was pale. "And

then he tried to set me up by dumping painkillers on the table in front of me. He wanted to send a photo to Maverick."

Her skin went cold. Blackmail was bad enough, but her first priority was Nick's health. "Where are the pills now?"

"I threw them out," he said, not meeting her eyes. "And Melissa caught Guy in the act, so it failed. It was a clumsy attempt."

"So everything's fine now? The blackmail attempt failed, and you didn't take the pills." Though she was clearly missing a piece of the puzzle, because there were divorce papers on the counter.

"But that's not the point," he said far too calmly for the conversation they were having. "I wanted to take them. Real bad."

She rubbed her fingertips over her temple. "But you didn't."

"You don't understand." He cleared his throat. "It made me face something. This is part of who I am, and it's not healthy to have this hanging over you and the babies. I won't let it affect you."

"Nick, I don't care," she said, finally giving up on trying to stay calm and allowing the desperation to leach into her voice. "Divorce isn't the answer."

"You said that as a SEAL I had to rely on everyone to do their jobs, and that's true, but sometimes as a leader I had to make the hard calls." His spine straightened, and his chin lifted a fraction. "And that's what I'm doing now. Stepping up. Making the hard call to keep everyone safe."

Angry now, she planted her hands on her hips. "Who made you the leader of our marriage? I thought we had a partnership. You don't get to make some sort of a noble sacrifice all on your own."

He didn't flinch from her anger. Didn't move a muscle. "You didn't see me when I was in the throes of the addiction. You and the babies are precious. I won't risk any possibility of that touching you and them."

Nothing seemed real—more like a bad dream or something happening to someone else. Or a practical joke in poor taste. He wasn't making this up—his body language showed no signs of deception. He honestly believed she'd be better off without him, despite this being so much bigger than the two of them.

"What about the babies? They need their father. What are you going to do?"

His eyes squeezed shut for long seconds before he met her gaze again. "They don't need a father like me around. If you need to go back to Connecticut, I understand. We can talk about visitation after they're born."

He pushed to his feet, and for the first time she noticed a bulging duffel bag on his other side. The air in the room seemed thicker as her lungs struggled to draw enough in.

She looked pointedly from the duffel bag back to him. "So you're leaving all three of us?"

"I'm a mess, Harper. You know that." He ran a hand down his face, then dug it into his pocket. "I need some space to decide how best to be a good father to all three kids. I want to get it right, as best I can."

This was all so very wrong. Yet how could she convince him how wrong it was when he'd already convinced himself otherwise?

At Nick's movements, Frank ambled over, probably hoping for a trip in the car.

"What about Frank?" she asked.

He leaned down to rub Frank's ears, and Frank grinned up at him. "He'll be better off here, with you. And the babies will love him."

He picked up the bag and hooked it over his shoulder. Waves of panic washed over her, making her cold.

"You're really going to walk out on me, Nick?" she asked, hardly believing she was saying those words aloud. "This can't be what you want."

"I'm fixing things. I might not like how I'm fixing it, but I can and I will." He crossed to her side, placed a lingering, chaste kiss on her forehead, then stepped back. "I'm freeing you."

Freeing her? She pinched the bridge of her nose. How was this even happening?

He took a step to the door, and she threw up a hand. "Hang on. This is your house. Why are you walking out? If you really want to separate, I'll go back to my place."

"No, stay as long as you need," he said simply. "I can't sit still right now anyway."

This was beyond crazy. "Where will you go?"

"I don't know." His forehead scrunched up, and he rubbed it with his free hand. "I'll stay at Natalie's

B&B tonight, and when I decide what I'll do after that, I'll let you know."

He took another step toward the door, and a sob crept up her throat. She only just managed to hold it back. "Nick, don't leave me."

"I'm sorry, Harper. Really sorry." And the look in his eyes said that was true. "I think this is the best thing to do."

He turned and walked through the door. Her husband, the man she loved, the father of her unborn babies, had just left her. Abandoned her. She covered her face with her hands as the sob in her throat finally broke free.

Twelve

Darkness...dark so thick and heavy it was choking... Fumbling for a light switch, but nothing... A flashlight... Thumbing the button... A beam of light... Illuminating nothing. Where was Harper? Swinging the beam in all directions... A newborn's cry... Frantically looking... Another cry joining the first... The babies! But where? There! In the distance... Harper carrying two babies... Yelling her name... She can't hear him... Walking away... No! His wife, his babies... Trying to run to catch them... Legs not working...stuck... Harper! His life, his everything, walking away... Harper! No...don't leave... Gone... Alone... Flashlight beam fading... Darkness...

Nick woke panting, covered in a cold sweat. He reached for Harper but only found empty sheets.

Memory came trickling back. She was in their bed, in their home, and he was here at the B&B alone. He didn't even have Frank to calm him.

Heart still racing double time, he kicked the sheet off.

"What the hell have I done?" he said to the empty room.

He'd left the best thing that had ever happened to him. Someone who made his life better just by being in it. Someone he wanted so badly he ached with it.

But leaving had never been about what he wanted. What he needed.

Leaving had been about what was best for Harper and the babies. He had to protect her, no matter the cost. And the cost was him.

He'd freed her to find someone who could meet her needs. Someone who wasn't messed up. Someone who wasn't him. A red-hot poker slammed into his chest at the thought.

His father's words came back to him. *"You're the strong one. You have to look after your mother and Malcolm."* If his father had met Harper, he would have included her in that group. And even if he hadn't, *Nick* included her in the group of people he was responsible for.

When you were the responsible one, sometimes you had to make sacrifices for them.

In the dark of an unfamiliar bedroom, snatches of memories and old dreams assailed him, of losing men in his unit. He'd been responsible for them, too, and he'd had to make hard calls for their sake. The familiar weight of grief and failure landed on him, smothering him. But this time, something was different. On the movie screen in his mind where the past had been stuck on a relentless loop, the scenes seemed to reorganize themselves. He'd replayed his options that day over and over in his mind and had never come up with a scenario where all his team survived. He'd always considered his lack of solution even in hindsight another failure. But now it hit him—if he hadn't made the hard call with his unit, more would have died. He'd made the best decision with the information, resources and options he had. Everyone had told him that, but it finally made sense. He finally believed it.

He didn't feel better—members of his unit had still died—but his heart was somehow a little less chaotic.

He said a silent prayer for those who'd been lost that day, and this time, he made a start at letting them go. Not to forget, never that, but to stop tormenting himself. He'd made the only decision possible that day. The price had been unspeakably high, but it was the best he could have done.

Now he needed to do the same with his marriage— hold fast now that he'd made the hard call to minimize casualties. A shudder ripped through him—his body revolting at what his mind knew was right.

If he could be granted one wish in this moment, he'd use it to have their family together. Harper, the babies, Ellie and him. But that would be selfish.

This sacrifice was his price to pay for their happiness, and for their sakes, he'd pay it a thousand times over.

All he had to do was learn how to keep breathing while he paid it.

Harper sat on the sofa in Nick's living room, watching the sun peep over the horizon and gradually reveal its full self. Despite the gorgeous view, her mind was still numb, and even her body felt only half there.

She'd spent the night in this one spot, unable to face the bed she'd shared with Nick now that she was alone, and equally unable to face leaving his home and severing that link to him. She'd checked her cell regularly in case he was trying to contact her, then while she had the cell in her hand, she'd searched the web for the effects of stress on unborn babies. It was another thing to worry about, but at least she was past the first three months, when the effects were worst. She rubbed her belly and tried some of the breathing exercises Nick had told her he used after his nightmares.

Frank had stayed with her and was now lying at the door, his head on his paws, staring forlornly, waiting for Nick to come home.

In the short time since they'd adopted Frank, he'd become devoted to Nick. It shouldn't have been surprising—while Harper had been at work, Nick and Frank had spent their days together. But it was more than that. They'd been helping each other heal.

"Frank," she said, but her voice was hoarse from

crying and the word was practically unrecognizable, so she tried again. "Frank."

This time he dragged his furry head up to look at her.

"Come over here, boy." She patted the sofa cushion beside her.

For long moments, his dark eyes simply contemplated her, then he stood, shook his body, ambled over and climbed up on the sofa. Harper lifted her arm so he could rest his head in her lap.

"I know," she said softly. "I miss him, too. But we'll be okay together." She laid a hand over the small mound of her stomach and rubbed Frank's ear with the other. "You, me and the babies. We'll be fine," she said, unsure if that was a lie or not.

Frank snuffled then let out a sigh. She sat with him, sharing comfort, until her tummy rumbled. She didn't feel like eating, but she needed to have something nutritious for her babies. With a final stroke of Frank's soft ear, she pushed to her feet and headed for the kitchen.

Fifteen minutes later, she'd made and drunk a smoothie and Frank had eaten a bowl of kibble.

She'd need to get ready for work soon, but she couldn't find the energy. A sleepless night and a bleak heart combined to steal all of her motivation, so she slumped onto the sofa again.

Frank glanced her way, then turned and trotted off down the hall, only to reappear a minute later, one of Nick's T-shirts in his mouth.

The sight brought tears to her eyes again. "Oh, Frank, come over here."

He and dropped the shirt at her feet. She wrapped her arms around his neck, letting her tears spill onto his fur. "I want him back, too."

The thing about being the one left behind was that as well as the grief about the ending, there was an overwhelming feeling of helplessness. That feeling had lurked inside her after her father had walked out on her and her mother, and it left her feeling paralyzed now.

Frank pulled his head from her grip and curled up on Nick's shirt at her feet. Her heart broke for him— his helplessness in the situation was as bad as hers.

She stilled. *As bad as hers?*

Something about that didn't seem right. *Frank* was powerless in the situation. She wasn't.

Yes, she'd been powerless as a child when her father abandoned her, but she'd worked hard over the years to become a confident person who was in charge of her own life. She drew in a long, shaky breath. She was still in charge of her own life.

Nick had ended their marriage because he'd made a decision about what was best. He was wrong. And she wasn't helpless, having to sit here and accept his view of how things should be.

She wasn't powerless.

It was time to take matters into her own hands and shape her own destiny.

After a quick shower, Harper was ready for action. She called Nick's cell, but it went to voice mail. The next few minutes of waiting to redial were spent trying to ignore the butterflies in her belly, but she got the recorded message again when she tried.

Not to be deterred now that she was taking charge of her own destiny, she called Natalie Valentine. Her friend picked up on the second ring.

"Cimarron Rose B&B, how can I help?"

"Natalie, it's Harper." She tried to sound casual despite her erratic pulse. "Is Nick there?"

"Hi, Harper," Natalie said. "Actually, no. He was here last night, but he left early."

She chewed her bottom lip. "I don't suppose he mentioned where he'd be today?"

"Not a word. He said last night he wouldn't want breakfast this morning then left early, before I was up. To be honest—" she paused, as if not sure how deliver bad news "—I'm not sure if he's coming back. He paid up front for one night."

Harper's heart missed a beat, but she sucked in a breath and steadied herself. He'd said he'd stay at the B&B until he made a plan, so maybe he'd spoken to Malcolm or his mother and decided to stay with them for a while. She straightened her shoulders. It might take a little longer than she'd hoped, but she'd find him. "Okay, thanks."

"Sorry I couldn't be more helpful," Natalie said, and Harper could imagine her friend's brows pinching together in concern.

"No, that's useful." She was already narrowing down the places he could be.

"And, Harper," Natalie said, her voice lowering,

"I'm not sure what's going on between you two, but whatever it is, I'm really sorry."

Harper wrapped a hand around her throat. "I appreciate that."

The next call was to Nick's brother. She dialed Malcolm's cell since he wouldn't be at work yet. He picked up on the first ring.

"Harper, how are—"

Before he could finish the greeting, she interrupted him. "Do you know where Nick is?"

"What's happened?" he asked, his voice suddenly serious.

Something about Nick's twin brother being worried sent a fresh wave of panic through her system. "I just have to find him."

"Harper," he said, sounding every inch the man who ran a large, successful company, "you need to tell me what happened."

"He left me," she said, trying to ignore the quaver in her voice.

"Oh, hell."

"So I guess he didn't come to you." It wasn't a question, but she needed to say it aloud, because now her best lead was gone.

"No." Malcolm swore under his breath. "And he's always had an uncanny knack for disappearing without a trace. Even when we were kids." There was rustling in the background, as if he was picking things up as he spoke. "I'll head out and check a few places. I'll call Mom on the way, too. Let me know if you find him."

"Thank you," she whispered, almost overwhelmed by his support.

"Harper, no matter what idiotic idea he's got in his head, you're good for each other. Remember that."

She managed to smile. "I will. Also, I won't be in to work today."

"Of course not. Just let me know when you find him."

"Sure," she said.

After disconnecting, she felt her shoulders slump. The only other place that was worth trying was the waterfall, so she grabbed her things, bundled Frank into the car and headed off. The journey seemed to take forever. The time had gone so quickly when Nick had first driven her out here, but now, desperate to reach her destination and her stomach churning with anxiety about how he'd be and what he'd think when he saw her, it was more like a journey of a thousand hours.

As she pulled into the parking lot, she glanced around, but Nick's car wasn't there.

"He's not here," she said to Frank, who stood up to look out the windshield the way he did whenever the car slowed down, hoping they'd arrived somewhere interesting.

She couldn't go back to the house. So what else could she do? She clipped Frank's leash on and walked over to the spot where they'd had their picnic. She let Frank sniff around for a while, then sank down on the grass and watched the waterfall.

She had no idea how long she'd been sitting there

when her cell rang. She answered quickly, hoping it was Malcolm with a lead, but it was Nick's number that flashed on her screen.

"Nick?"

"Where are you?" he asked, and she closed her eyes, savoring his deep, smooth voice.

"At the waterfall." She opened her eyes again to glance around at his favorite spot. "Where are you?"

"Home, looking for you." His voice gave nothing away. "Wait where you are. I'm coming to you."

After the call disconnected, she quickly called Malcolm to let him know he could stop searching, and then paced around the grassy area, letting Frank sniff all the smells he could find, trying to keep herself occupied so she didn't implode. He could be coming to discuss a divorce and access to the babies. Maybe he wanted to get back together. Or maybe there was even worse news that he couldn't deliver over the phone.

She was sitting on the grass, Frank resting beside her, when she first caught a glimpse of Nick rounding the corner and heading her way. Frank took off, his leash trailing behind him, and leaped on his human, resting his paws on Nick's chest. Nick took a minute to properly greet his dog, talking to him and rubbing his ears, then looked up. His gaze snagged hers, and goose bumps raced across her skin.

He walked toward her, his expression still giving nothing away. But his steps were sure. Her heart beat unevenly and roughly against her ribs, and she had no idea what to say or do. She stood, brushing off the grass from her pants, and offered him half a smile.

She wanted to crawl into his embrace and hold on as tight as she could, but they didn't have that relationship anymore, so instead she simply waited until he reached her.

He stopped just beyond touching distance and cleared his throat. "Hi."

"Hi." She looked down at Frank, who was still bounding around, happy to have them all in the one place again, then back to him.

"Are you okay?" he asked.

"Fine," she said, lying. "You?"

"Fine." He gave her half a smile, clearly lying as well. "Harper, I need to ask. Do you hate me?"

Hate him? Not even close. "No."

"I walked out on you, even though you told me on the day we got engaged that it was a trigger for you."

She nodded slowly. "Yeah, you did that."

"I'm more sorry than I can say about that." His gaze was fathomless. "You should hate me for it."

She'd always known she'd made bad choices in past relationships, practically setting herself up to be left behind. Nick was different.

She lifted one shoulder and let it drop. "And yet, I don't."

"Then I have another question," he said, everything about him solemn. "Do you love me?"

She'd been so excited to tell him yesterday that she'd realized she loved him—it would have been a joyous moment. This wasn't the way she'd pictured it going at all, but she couldn't lie. "Yes," she said. "I love you."

He nodded as if he'd been expecting that. "And I love you so much it's tearing me up inside."

Those were words she'd been desperate to hear, and yet they didn't make her heart sing, because she still had no idea where he was going with this. "Why did you want to see me, Nick?"

"Were you serious when you said my addiction doesn't matter to you?"

"Absolutely," she said without hesitation.

His brows drew together, and he looked over at the waterfall for endless seconds before clearing his throat. "I realized something today."

She was almost too scared to ask but couldn't help herself. "What's that?"

"Growing up, we weren't close to my aunts and uncles, so the only marriage I saw close up was my parents'."

"Which sounds like it was perfect." It wasn't just the way he'd spoken of his parents, but it had shone brightly in his mother's eyes when she'd mentioned her husband at their wedding.

"I wouldn't say it was perfect, but it was certainly a good one." A faraway smile flitted across his face. "They were devoted to each other."

She sighed, glad there were people in the world who were able to live out the fairy tale. "They were lucky."

He tilted his head in acknowledgment. "And your parents' marriage was—"

"A disaster," she supplied so he didn't have to say it. "Even before my father left."

"So, what I realized is that since you and I said

our vows, I've been trying to live up to my father's example of being a perfect husband and you've been worried that we'll turn out like your parents and I'll leave you."

She stilled, absorbing that, and realized it was completely true. She pulled her hair back from her face, then let it drop. "That's a fair amount of baggage. Maybe we were always going to fail."

He cupped the side of her face. "We just needed a clean slate and different vows."

"What do you mean?"

"I've been trying to make everything perfect. Fix things for everyone. For you. But it didn't need to be perfect, to be *right*. It just needed to be *us*." He took her hands in his. "The thing is, even though I'll do my best never to give in to painkillers again, I'm never going to be a perfect husband. And I don't want a perfect marriage. That's like wanting a fantasy, not a real relationship."

He reached into his pocket and withdrew a small box, then opened it to reveal two gold bands. He took one out and laid it on the flat of his palm.

"Here are my new vows," he said, meeting her gaze squarely. "I choose you, Harper Lake, to be my wife. Not because you're carrying my babies, and not because I'm expecting you to be a perfect wife. I choose you because instead of being scared of my darkness, you were patient and persistent and you got me a dog."

She hiccupped a laugh, and he reached for her hand with his free one and intertwined their fingers.

"I love that you overcame your preference for privacy at work and held my hand in front of all of your colleagues. I love that you tried so hard to bond with Ellie. And I especially love that you stood by me each time the darkness tried to carry me away."

Tears welled in her eyes, and she brushed at them before they could fall. The rest of the world faded away, and all she could see was Nick. He was magnificent, and she couldn't imagine ever loving anyone the way she loved him.

"If you choose me today, I vow that I'll always try to make you happy. And even when my demons whisper to me, I vow that I'll never give up on you. On us."

He offered her the gold ring on his palm, and she nodded once, so he slipped it on her ring finger next to the first gold band he'd given her. Beyond words, she reached up and found his mouth, found his kiss. She melted into him, wanting the kiss, the moment, to never end.

Eventually, he pulled back. "Harper," he rasped.

When she'd regained her breath, she picked out the other gold ring from the box in his hand and held it on her upturned palm. Then she looked into his eyes and finally gave her love free rein.

"I choose you, Nick Tate, to be my husband. Not because you're the father of our babies, and not because I'm expecting you to be a perfect husband. I choose you because I love your noble heart. I love the way you love Ellie. I love that you jumped on board with my plan to rescue Frank before you even knew the details. I love that the people under your command still matter so much to you. I love that even though we disagree on things, you always have my best interests at heart."

He lifted her hand and brushed his lips across the tops of her fingers.

"If you choose me today, I vow that even though I'll always want you to be as happy as you can, I'll accept you as you are, with all your glorious imperfections. And I know there will be bumps along the road for us, but I vow to never give up on you."

She slipped the ring on his finger, and the sight of it there with all the extra meaning of these vows made the tears that had been welling in her eyes finally burst free. He pulled her to him, cradling her against his chest, and whispered, "I promise you, Harper. I'll never give up on us."

"Neither will I," she said.

Frank appeared and tried to stick his snout between them to work out what the noise was, but gave up and flopped down at their feet.

With a finger, Nick tipped Harper's face up so he could see her eyes. "By the power invested in me by—" he glanced around "—Frank the Labrador, I now pronounce us husband and wife. For real this time."

"For real this time," she echoed and smiled.

And then he kissed his bride.

* * * * *

If you're on Twitter, tell us what you think
of Harlequin Desire! #harlequindesire

COMING NEXT MONTH FROM

Available August 8, 2017

#2533 THE CEO'S NANNY AFFAIR
Billionaires and Babies • by Joss Wood
When billionaire Linc Ballantyne's ex abandons not one, but *two* children, he strikes up a wary deal with her too-sexy sister. She'll be the nanny and they'll keep their hands to themselves. But their temporary truce soon becomes a temporary tryst!

#2534 TEMPTED BY THE WRONG TWIN
Texas Cattleman's Club: Blackmail • by Rachel Bailey
Harper Lake is pregnant, but the father isn't who she thinks—it's her boss's identical twin brother! Wealthy former Navy SEAL Nick Tate pretended to be his brother as a favor, and now he's proposing a marriage of convenience that just might lead to real romance...

#2535 THE TEXAN'S BABY PROPOSAL
Callahan's Clan • by Sara Orwig
Millionaire Texan Marc Medina must marry immediately to inherit his grandfather's ranch. When his newly single secretary tells him she's pregnant, he knows a brilliant deal when he sees one. He'll make her his wife...and have her in his bed!

#2536 LITTLE SECRETS: CLAIMING HIS PREGNANT BRIDE by Sarah M. Anderson
Restless—that's businessman and biker Seth Bolton. But when he rescues pregnant runaway bride Kate Burroughs, he wants much more than he should with the lush mom-to-be... But she won't settle for anything less than taming his heart!

#2537 FROM TEMPTATION TO TWINS
Whiskey Bay Brides • by Barbara Dunlop
When Juliet Parker goes home to reopen her grandfather's restaurant, she clashes with her childhood crush, tycoon Caleb Watford, who's building a rival restaurant. Then the stakes skyrocket after their one night leaves her expecting two little surprises!

#2538 THE TYCOON'S FIANCÉE DEAL
The Wild Caruthers Bachelors • by Katherine Garbera
Derek Caruthers promised his best friend that their fake engagement would end after he'd secured his promotion...but what's a man of honor to do when their red-hot kisses prove she's the only one for him?

Get 2 Free Books,
Plus 2 Free Gifts—
just for trying the Reader Service!

HARLEQUIN *Desire*

HDI7R2

SPECIAL EXCERPT FROM

HQN™

Ready or not, love will find a way,
even when confronted with the most reluctant of hearts...

Read on for a sneak peek of the next
GUTHRIE BROTHERS *book, WORTH THE WAIT,*
from New York Times *bestselling author Lori Foster!*

Violet, looking messier than Hogan had ever seen her, was leaning over the papers again scattered across her desk.

"Violet?"

Slowly she turned her face toward him.

Her bloodshot eyes surprised him. Sick. He stepped in farther. "Hey, you okay?"

She looked from him to the paperwork. "I don't know." More coughs racked her.

Hogan strode forward and put a hand to her forehead. "Shit. You're burning up."

"What time is it?"

"A few minutes after midnight."

"Oh." She pushed back from the desk but didn't make it far. "The restaurant," she gasped in between strained breaths.

"I took care of it." Holding her elbow, he helped to support her as she stood. His most pressing thought was getting her home and in bed. No, not the way he'd like, but definitely the way she needed. "Where are your car keys?"

Unsteady on her feet, she frowned. "What do you mean, you took care of it?"

"You have good employees—you know that. They're aware of the routine. Colt pitched in, too. Everything is done."

"But..."

"I double-checked. I'm not incompetent, so trust me."

Her frown darkened.

"You can thank me, Violet."

She tried to look stern, coughed again and gave up. "Thank you." Still she kept one hand on the desk. "I'm just so blasted tired."

"I know." He eased her into his side, his arm around her. "Come on. Let me drive you home." Then he found her purse and without a qualm, dug through it for her keys.

He found them. He also found two condoms. His gaze flashed to hers, but her eyes were closed and she looked asleep on her feet, her body utterly boneless as she drew in shallow, strained breaths.

"Come on." With an arm around her, her purse and keys held in his free hand, he led her out the back way to the employee lot, securing the door behind her. Her yellow Mustang shone bright beneath security lights.

His bike would be okay. Or at least, it better be.

Violet tried to get herself together but it wasn't easy. She honestly felt like she could close her eyes and nod right off. "The trash—"

"Was taken out." He opened the passenger door and helped her in.

"If you left on even one fan—"

"It would set off the security sensors. I know. They're all off." He fastened her seat belt around her and closed her door.

As soon as he slid behind the wheel, she said, "But the end-of-day reports—"

"Are done." He started her car. "Try not to worry, okay?"

Easier said than done.

Because the town was so small, Hogan seemed to know where she lived even though she'd never had him over. She hadn't dared.

Hogan in her home? Nope. Not a good idea.

Even feeling miserable, her head pounding and her chest aching, she was acutely aware of him beside her in the enclosed car, and the way he kept glancing at her. He tempted her, always had, from the first day she'd met him.

He was also a major runaround. Supposedly a reformed runaround, but she didn't trust in that. Things had happened with his late wife, things that had made him bitter and unpredictable.

Yet no less appealing.

She wasn't one to pry; otherwise she might have gotten all the details from Honor, his sister-in-law, already. She figured if he ever wanted to, Hogan himself would tell her. Not that there was any reason, since she would not get involved with him.

Hogan was fun to tease, like watching the flames in a bonfire. You watched, you enjoyed, but you did not jump in the fire. She needed Hogan Guthrie, but she wasn't a stupid woman, so she tried to never court trouble.

Don't miss WORTH THE WAIT
by New York Times *bestselling author Lori Foster!*

EXCLUSIVE LIMITED TIME OFFER AT
www.HARLEQUIN.com

$15.99 U.S./$19.99 CAN.

$1.⁵⁰ OFF

New York Times Bestselling Author

LORI FOSTER

worth the wait

Ready or not...
love will find a way

Available July 25, 2017.
Get your copy today!

Receive **$1.50 OFF** the purchase price of
WORTH THE WAIT by Lori Foster
when you use the coupon code below on Harlequin.com.

LFWORTHIT

Offer valid from July 25, 2017, until August 31, 2017, on www.Harlequin.com.

Valid in the U.S.A. and Canada only. To redeem this offer, please add the print
or ebook version of WORTH THE WAIT by Lori Foster to your shopping cart and
then enter the coupon code at checkout.

HQN™
www.HQNBooks.com

PHCOUPLFHD0817

LOVE
Harlequin
romance?

Join our Harlequin community to share your thoughts and connect with other romance readers!

Be the first to find out about promotions, news, and exclusive content!

Sign up for the Harlequin e-newsletter and download a free book from any series at

www.TryHarlequin.com

CONNECT WITH US AT:

Harlequin.com/Community

 Facebook.com/HarlequinBooks

 Twitter.com/HarlequinBooks

 Instagram.com/HarlequinBooks

 Pinterest.com/HarlequinBooks

ReaderService.com

**ROMANCE WHEN
YOU NEED IT**

HSOCIAL2017

Jonas was impeccably dressed.

Kat's eyes traveled over a broad chest and wide shoulders, up a tanned neck to a strong jaw covered with two-day-old stubble. A mouth that was slow to smile but still sexy. Rich, successful and hot.

He had a rep for being a bit of a bastard, in business and in bed. That fact only dropped his sexy factor by a quarter of a percent.

"Mr. Halstead, welcome back to El Acantilado," Kat murmured, ignoring her jumping heart.

"Call me Jonas."

It wasn't the first time he'd made the offer, but Kat had no intention of accepting. It wasn't professional, and formality kept a healthy distance between her and guys in fancy suits. Like her ex-husband, and sadly, just like her father, those kinds of men were not to be trusted.

But it really annoyed Kat that a thousand sparks danced on her skin as Jonas's smile turned his face in her mind from remote-but-still-hot to oh-my-God-I want-to-rip-his-clothes-off.

No. Sexy billionaires were *not* her type. She'd married, and divorced, a ruthless and merciless rich guy.

But it sure felt like she had the screaming hots for a man she shouldn't.

And it was all Jonas Halstead's fault.

Don't miss
CONVENIENT CINDERELLA BRIDE
by Joss Wood,
available September 2017 wherever
Harlequin® Desire books and ebooks are sold.

www.Harlequin.com

Inspirational Romance to Warm Your Heart and Soul

Brides of Lost Creek:
In Amish country, all roads lead to weddings

Widower Caleb King is set on raising his two
small children without assistance from anyone—
especially a relative of the wife who abandoned
them. When Caleb is injured, Jessie Miller is just
as determined to help her late cousin's family—
never imagining that coming into their lives
could lead to her own happily-ever-after.

Don't miss

Second Chance
Amish Bride
by
Marta Perry

Available September 2017
wherever Love Inspired books
and ebooks are sold.

 www.Facebook.com/LoveInspiredBooks

 www.Twitter.com/LoveInspiredBks

www.LoveInspired.com

ISBN-13:978-0-373-83861-5

83861

UPC

0 65373 51029 7

LIMPIBC0817

Desire

Mistaken identity leads to suddenly expecting...only from *USA TODAY* bestselling author Rachel Bailey!

Harper Lake can't believe she bedded her boss after a wild night at a masked ball. But then she finds out it was actually his identical twin, Nick Tate! *And* she's carrying his babies!

With his own set of twins on the way, Nick knows that proposing to Harper is the only next step. Yet the former navy SEAL is battling some deeply buried demons. Welcoming Harper back into his bed is the easy part. Finding true love and wedded bliss will be the ultimate test...and temptation.

$5.25 U.S./$5.99 CAN.

ISBN-13: 978-0-373-83861-5

50525

CATEGORY
PASSION

HARLEQUIN®
DESIRE

harlequin.com

9 780373 838616